Adriana

LESLIE HACHTEL

Also Available from Leslie Hachtel
Romantic Suspense
Texas Summer
Payback
Once Upon a Tablecloth
Memories Never Die

Notorious Series
Murder Most Notorious

The Dance Series
The Dream Dancer
Emma's Dance
The Jester's Dance
A Dance in Time

The Morocco Series
Bound to Morocco
Tied to Morocco
Freed from Morocco

Historical
The Defiant Bride
Hannah's War

Crossover Contemporary/Historical/Time Travel
Stay With Me
Come Back To Me

Acknowledgements

As always, my sincere thanks and gratitude to Jena Brignola, a genius when it comes to creating perfect covers.

And to Judi Fennell, without whose talents I would be lost.

And to my ever wonderful proof reader, Bob, who cleans up my act.

And to you, my readers. Thank you so much for sharing my stories with me!

Table of Contents

Chapter One

Adriana Booth crouched between the tall, formidable shipping containers. The mingled odors of sea and fish, oil and sweat assailed her senses and she tried not to inhale through her nose. The mocking clouds obscured the moonlight and the damp cold crept through to her very bones. Her fingers were numb and she rubbed them briskly to regain some circulation. The biting tang of the salt air was so much sharper here on the docks than the beloved soft, damp earth scent surrounding her home, which had only been freshened by hints of the encroaching sea. A wave of nausea threatened, but she forced it down.

Adriana reached back to massage the tightness in her neck. The touch of her icy hand did nothing to aid the cramping. How long had she been squeezed into this small space? Hours? It felt more like days. She dropped her hand and inadvertently brushed against her left shoulder. The persistent ache was a reminder of why she was here in the dark like some terrified creature. Yes that was what she had been reduced to, a frightened little mouse. It was sickening. Now, with patience wearing thin, she tapped her fingers against the huge, looming crate in front of her. The wood was so rough. She ran her

1

hand along the surface and was recompensed with a sliver of wood embedding into the skin. She wanted to scream as she dug the hateful thing out with her teeth.

The dock was still bustling. Some men dressed in suits passed by, some alone, some in groups of two and three, without a break. Would there never be an opportunity to move forward?

Some of the vessels were preparing to cast off and the sounds of their ropes unwinding increased the feeling of frustration and urgency. Adriana was ready to take her chances at discovery when a single set of footsteps approached from behind her hiding place. An errant shaft of moonlight lit the man's face as he passed. Breath caught in her throat as his features were illuminated. Dark hair, a strong jaw, a finely chiseled mouth. His coat stretched across broad shoulders and muscles stood in vivid relief against his hose, just visible above shiny black boots. Moving with the air of one ever in charge, he was the most handsome man she'd ever beheld. This was a man who would have stood out among any suitors.

It took a moment to recover and by then he was nearly out of sight. Unwittingly, she had leaned forward to get a better view, then quickly tucked herself back in place before she lost her balance. Suddenly, he stopped. Had he seen her? Her pulse quickening, she made herself small and controlled her breathing. A man's voice echoed across the docks. The word 'Captain'. Adriana could not hear the remainder of the exchange, but the handsome man nodded, then walked further away from her. Which ship was his? Miraculously, all seemed quiet now and she inched forward, squinting in the darkness to try and discern the answer.

"Get out of the way, old woman," a man shouted at her.

Nearly jumping out of her skin, she skittered back into the shadows, stubbing her toes on a crate. She was beginning to hate these boxes.

A parade of filthy, barefoot men marched by, the steady rhythm of their movements interlaced with the clatter of chains echoing in the dark. A shiver came unbidden and she wondered as to the offenses that brought them here, their futures controlled by others. Not so different from her own circumstances. It was so wrong to be here instead of home, dressing for the evening, primping after a scented bath. There should be suitors' praises instead of strange men yelling at her, though this disguise was a far cry from her usual fancy gowns. Adriana shifted her weight, bumping her left side against an unyielding surface. Again was the reminder of the pain in her shoulder, a constant prod that Sarah Jane wanted her dead. Adriana should have sought her out and confronted her stepmother, or worse. But that Adriana existed no more. The missile coming out of nowhere, shattering the glass in the library window, had sunk into her flesh, but also into her soul. It had made her afraid. She slammed her right fist into the left, the pain shooting up her arm and taking her mind off her bruised foot and sore shoulder.

Now, shaking with dread and anticipation and excitement, she only wanted to be on his ship. The voice had come from the left, narrowing options.

The initial thought of sneaking aboard as a stowaway had been foolish, at best. Spending an entire voyage, maybe months, scrambling for food and other necessities would be impossible. As would time spent in a dark, secreted place without light or fresh air. She might no longer be brave, but she would not add insult to injury. The newest idea, to use the skills learned since childhood, now definitely seemed a much better prospect. She simply had to remain calm and be confident in her disguise and abilities. All those tutors when she was growing up and it was the family cook, Cassie, whose knowledge would serve her now.

The foggy mists wrapped around her skirts like tendrils, breathing with the wind. Its touch was like a living thing, pushing here and there and offering no answers as to direction. The lapping of the water against the ships was a siren song, soothing and whispering promise of things to come. She closed her eyes and let the melody ease her frayed nerves.

Adriana opened her eyes again to study the ships in the harbor, tall and imposing. Some looked like ancient dragons born to slay the sea. Others squatted across the water, their holds so much larger they looked like fat hens spreading out to protect what was theirs, their masts keeping watch. The line of ships all swayed together with the rhythm of a heartbeat, mindful it was always to be the ocean in control. The men who sailed these ships knew that. To forget that the sea was mistress was to die.

She slipped from one shadow to another, trying not to inhale the pungent air, desperate to quell rising fears. She chided herself for the nerves. She had fled the prospect of her demise knowing almost anywhere would be more welcoming than home. The bullet to the shoulder had ended naiveté quickly. Adriana would never forgive her stepmother for taking away the feeling of safety.

Still enveloped in the pools of darkness, the hood of the dark cloak raised to conceal most of her face, the hours had progressed slowly and finally, the activity on the docks began to diminish. She scratched her stomach and rubbed her arms under the rough muslin garment she wore. The thing had been found in the attic and seemed a perfect choice at the time, but she was now wondering. Perhaps she was not alone in the clothing and myriad tiny creatures populated it, too. Shuddering at the thought, she put it out of mind. There were enough worries at the moment and simply no room for more.

The old gown made her think of other dresses, other times. Times when life was full of parties and she loved being the center of attention. That life seemed so long ago.

The tars were moving from the streets now, laughing loudly from too much ale and bawdy jokes, holding tightly to the doxies they had chosen to warm their beds this night. Another garish waterfront whore appeared. This one grabbed hold of a sailor already occupied. She fondled his chest when the man's original companion took offense and pushed back. There was a small scuffle and the three came to terms. All then moved off together as they half-walked half-swayed-down the street, the sailor grabbing first one by the breast and then the other.

The area was very quiet now. It was now or never, before her courage totally abandoned her. Many ships caught her attention as her gaze swept the left side of the harbor. Her one eye was concealed by the black patch which irritated her skin and lessened her ability to see more broadly, but one vessel stood out. It sat otherworldly in the soft moonlit light, its huge masts kissing the sky. It did not matter what it was about this particular vessel that was intriguing. This ship was brazen and sleek and built for speed. Adriana convinced herself it was her captain's. Surely, it was the right one.

With newly acquired, though limited, knowledge, it appeared to be a cargo ship carrying goods rather than human bounty. No dark hold full of misery and waste. It

5

would transport some passengers as well as be an agent for goods. Based on the size of her, Adriana judged the crew should number about eighty. *Windstar* it declared boldly in white letters, the fading moonlight pausing long enough to highlight the proud name emblazoned in white on her side.

Sliding along the slick surface of the wooden quay, she looked about for any sign of life on the deck. Certainly it would not be completely deserted, even at this time of night. Someone would most definitely be standing guard.

"Who goes there?" a voice demanded and she jumped at the sound. She had expected to be challenged, but was unprepared all the same. Adriana nearly fell on the drenched slats. She gasped, but was thrilled to recognize the same voice that had called for 'her' captain. On the deck, a man stepped into a sliver of light. He was tall, with very broad shoulders and a jagged, nasty scar that made a crisscross pattern on his left cheek. giving him the air of danger. He looked to be two score, but strong, and she instinctively, despite his appearance, felt this was a man who would listen to reason. He peered directly at her, visibly relaxed with legs spread wide apart, then leaned forward on the rail crossing his arms at the wrists.

"Well, good evening, old woman. What are you doing about at this hour? 'Tis not safe, you know."

"Is this your ship?" she asked, sure the answer would be no.

"Why is it your business? Do you require something?"

"I—need work. I was hoping you could use a cook. I am an excellent one. I have a liking for the sea and require a job. Please?"

The man looked down at her. Adriana knew that her appearance conveyed an almost pitiful vision in a patched

6

and dirty gown. The dark cotton dress hung overlarge on her small frame. The black patch over her left eye must have given her a strange look—like the shadow of a very old pirate come back from the dead to haunt the waterfront.

"Sorry, old woman." The man started away.

"Wait, please."

He stopped and turned back. "Well?"

"Sir, it is not a concern that I would tempt your men." She indicated her appearance. "I can do more with your meager rations than anyone. You shall feast like kings and I will wager the men will give you more work with their bellies happily full." She had heard that sailors rarely had enough to eat on the journey across the sea and what they did have was barely palatable.

"I see. You found yourself in trouble, I suppose. Is the law after ya? Is that it? Did you steal? Or worse, kill someone?"

She winced, but recovered. "Do I appear to be a dangerous criminal to you, sir?"

He laughed. "No. I think not. But you must have a reason to want to go to sea. So, if you want to tell me the truth…"

"Would you believe I seek adventure in my old age?" She looked up at him pleadingly.

The light from the dying moon suddenly waxed bright and she could see his features more clearly. He seemed to find her compelling, or perhaps he could not resist a damsel in distress, even if she appeared older than his mother.

"How did ya know our last cook died?"

"I—did not know. Did you kill him?" she asked, innocently.

He laughed out loud. "It is possible the crew might have. He could not tell a piece of meat from leather or a biscuit from a bit of rope."

It was pure luck this ship was in need of a cook.

"Well," he grumbled, after what seemed an interminable wait, "I will have to check with the captain, a course. Maybe later than sooner, though. He might not like the idea of a woman on the crew, but then again…" He chuckled softly. "There would be no privacy for you."

"I could sleep in the galley and see to my own needs without troubling anyone," she responded with bravado. "Please, sir. I need the work."

He was quiet for a moment. "Well, it seems I am in a generous mood this night. I will seriously consider your proposal, but only under certain conditions."

"Done," she responded, trying to contain her excitement, as their dealings were not yet concluded.

"You have yet to hear my terms."

"I am certain they will be acceptable." She smiled broadly, hoping to show a willingness to cooperate. "Whatever they are, I shall abide by them gladly."

"Ah, to hear those words from a wench. No matter. Come closer."

She obeyed and he squinted at her, giving her a moment of concern. "My name is Tate."

"Mary." It was the first name that came to mind. Her own was dangerously distinctive.

"Well, Mary, I am the captain's man. I have spent most of my life on the sea. The last five have been with this captain. I can tell you he is a fine man. I know he would be happy if you prove yourself and none have lost weight on this trip. To say nothing of keeping the passengers appeased. Most manage to do no more than complain. Without a cook, it was to be a problem. So, I am taking you at your word, now, that you know your way around a galley and are experienced at feeding so many."

"Yes, Mr. Tate, I can indeed cook. I took the liberty of bringing a sample or two." She took a few quick steps toward the hiding place on the dock, then slowed, remembering her age. She would have to be more careful. Adriana retrieved a basket covered with a cloth and a small bundle. Stretching her arms as high as they would reach allowed him access to the hamper. He leaned over and scooped up the basket. Another bundle she kicked between her feet.

"I spent the last few days helping out at the local inn and baked these this morning using only bit of flour, honey, and cinnamon. Tell me what you think." She smiled. Planning so carefully had been wise.

Tate chose a scone from the basket. He bit into it and licked his lips. "Even without cream or jam… it is good." He finished the last bite and grinned. "You have convinced me. Listen well, then, to the details of our agreement. First, you must remain unseen by the captain until he has tested your fare. If you have deceived me, it will stir his ire and I will bear the brunt. That man has a temper to behold. Or better, not to behold." Tate clearly enjoyed his own humor. Adriana held her tongue. "So, if that is the case, I will personally see you thrown overboard."

She wondered for a moment if he would consider making good on that threat, and decided he could not. He was watching her closely and she smiled, trying to convince him of her skills and her sincerity.

"I warn you now, there will be no special privileges for ya." He clearly tried to sound gruff, but he was melting like butter on a hot summer afternoon. He hesitated, thinking, then obviously deciding. "I don't suppose the old superstition would apply. After all, one of the passengers is a woman." This he said almost to himself. She was hoping the man was assured that the old irrational belief of bad luck associated with having a woman aboard would not be a hindrance here. One could probably ignore the fact that she was a female at all in this guise.

"I do appreciate what you are doing for me, Mr. Tate. I shall not require any special treatment and I assure you I will more than prove my worth. I promise, you shall not be sorry for this."

"Fine, Mary. Now, where are your things? I take it you have some belongings with you?"

"Just what I have in this." Adriana pointed to the small bundle at her feet.

"Get yourself aboard then and I will give you a quick tour. We sail on the tide." Tate hesitated, then turned back to her. "You did not ask what port we sailed for. Care you not?"

Mary smiled at him. "Nay. Just to sea and whatever fate has in store."

"You are a brave and foolhardy woman. Or perhaps, more desperate than any one of your years has right to be. Come along then. Oh, and we sail for the colonies. Williamsburg, Virginia to be exact."

Mary was thrilled. The colonies. A punishment for some, a boon to others. A new world. Smiling, she grabbed the sack and scrambled up the ramp to the deck. Now was not the time to give in to any form of feminine weakness or inner disputes. She followed him below decks toward the galley. The dark walls smelled of salt and sea and Adriana's heart pumped with excitement. She pressed her lips together lest she appear too overeager.

They walked down a very narrow, dark corridor to a door that opened onto a large space.

The galley was well designed, compact, the main feature being the cast iron hearth, attached to the chimney that led up through the smoke sail. There was space to work and sufficient utensils in evidence to make the job easier.

Suddenly, she was seized with panic. What if she could not perform her duties? What if she broke down and huddled in a heap in the corner drowning in tears? The reality of seeing the kitchen presented a vision into the next weeks and it was terrifying. Her stomach knotted like a too tight spring. She clenched her fists at her sides, then pulled determination up from her very toes and scolded herself to stop whining. Adriana raised her eyes back to the galley and it was suddenly a manageable thing, a challenge to overcome, and she promised herself she would be up to the task.

To the right was a large storage area lined with shelves. Tucked into a corner was a small cot. There was barely enough room to turn around in there. It was packed with supplies, and seemed terribly close and stuffy. Even back here, cooking smells had permeated the wooden slats in the walls and years of grease had left its marks in splotchy designs, unappetizing at best. But Adriana thought, it will have to do.

He had waited, perhaps for complaint and, when none was forthcoming, a slight smile lifted his mouth. She knew then she had convinced him. That she was willing to pay her way with hard work. Now, all that remained was deliver on her promise. Yes, only that.

"Thank you, Mr. Tate. I am truly grateful and I will not disappoint."

"And it's just Tate. We carry eighty, including passengers. No human cargo. Captain does not believe in that. Breakfast had best be ready each day by sunrise or you will be swimming back to the shore." Then, he was gone.

Mary smiled and moved her bundle into the corner. She nearly laughed out loud at the thought of its contents. Tate had seen a poor, old beggar lady. A velvet dress and silk chemise for when she arrived at her destination. And, if only the man knew she had enough money and jewels on her person to buy this ship several times over. There were other secrets, as well, but revealing those could get her killed.

She did a quick inventory of the supplies and was impressed by the stores at hand. The pantry shelves were bursting. There was butter and rice, dried vegetables, flour, and honey. There were dried herbs and coffee and tea. And she was sure the hold contained live chickens and hogs. That would mean eggs as well as fresh meat. She prayed another would see to the slaughtering. For today, there was salt beef already soaking to remove the brine and some hard tack biscuits. Hopefully, this would be easier than she had anticipated. Cassie had taught her to cook for the household, so how much more difficult could it be to expand the amount to serve more?

Adriana reached into the folds of her old cotton dress and withdrew several small sacks filled with coins. In the lining of her heavy cloak there were necklaces, bracelets, and rings worth a small fortune, along with more tightly packed coins. Tucking her bundles under the cot, she covered herself with her cloak. The creaking of the boards matching her breathing, she fell into an exhausted sleep. There was perhaps only an hour or two to rest, but it would have to suffice.

Chapter Two

Adriana was rudely awakened by shouting and strange, unrecognizable noises. Instinctively, she reached out with eyes half closed to open the bed drapes, but they were not there. She sat straight up and looked about, trying to get her bearings. The aching creak of the vessel as it yielded to its mistress brought her back. She prayed she had not slept overlong. It was still dark and none were calling for her so she relaxed. She slowly rose from the cot, planting her feet on the shifting floor. Stretching and easing the sore muscles along her spine, she folded her cloak and laid it on top of the small bags concealing her wealth.

In another time, early morning would see her mounting her mare just as the sky was painting itself with oranges and pinks and blues. Together, they would fly across the emerald carpet, inhaling the lush fragrances bursting forth, instead of the stale odors emitting from a well-used kitchen.

With no mirror at hand, Adriana reached up to touch the eye patch and adjust the scarf on her head. Satisfied, she stepped into the galley. Blinking away sleep, she focused on the task at hand. Among the supplies was a bushel of apples. Fruits of any kind were rare on a ship and highly prized, so she would see that they were served only to the officers and passengers. She tested one of the sea biscuits and grimaced. They were hard and tasteless. That was reassuring. If the crew had grown accustomed to this food, almost anything she prepared would be welcomed. A gravy made from the dried beef would certainly make the biscuits more palatable. The apples would gain flavor from some cinnamon and honey. There were also potatoes. Menu planning kept her thoughts focused on the work and away from too much thinking of other things. She wondered who to ask about eggs.

Hoping for some water, she was pleased to see someone had brought several large buckets and lined them against the far wall. The scent of the rum that was mixed in to make the water safe to drink caused her nose to wrinkle with distaste. She missed the sweet scent of orange blossoms that flavored desserts at home and wafted about the kitchen.

With the impressive array and variety of foodstuffs, Adriana had known almost immediately that this ship was wealthier than most. The captain must be demanding or the passengers important. This captain. Her captain. What if she were standing at the head of the stairs dressed in that favorite red satin dress with the crystal beads that sparkled? He would notice her then, and surely seek her favors. Ah, but in this disguise…

Well, daydreaming was for those without eighty men to feed.

Kindling had been laid in the fireplace and the flint awaited. It took what seemed like a hundred strikes before the wood caught, died, and caught again. She fanned the flames until they were bright. Not as easy as she had thought. She hefted one of the buckets, poured it into two waiting pots and went about peeling potatoes and chopping fruit. While she worked, the ship rocked and lurched as it

14

caught the tide and made its way toward the ocean. Several times, she had to grab hold of a shelf or the wall. She would need to develop sea legs or suffer the consequences. Being on water was not foreign, but experience had been limited to the Thames. Would it feel the same on the open sea?

As the water boiled and the food simmered in smaller pots above the fire, Adriana took a moment to locate the eating areas. Across the walkway, redolent from many men, the two dining rooms sat adjacent. The first was for the officers and passengers. The round table was made of walnut and the chairs had new looking padding. The second room was more stark with a worn, square table decorated with scratches and water stains. The seats were rough wooden benches that stretched out on each of the four sides. Would she be expected to serve, too? She hurried back to the galley and wondered where the dishes were stored. A secured cabinet on the far side, above where the water buckets had been set, contained the stacked crockery. She hefted a plate. It was heavy and not easily broken. She could only imagine what rough treatment it must get. She was replacing it on the counter when there was a shuffling sound behind her.

She turned to see Tate leaning against the doorway, watching. "So, I see you're up and about. That is a good sign. The passengers are just settling in and will be wanting breakfast. As will the rest of us. You need not worry over serving the food. A cabin boy is on the way and he'll take out the platters. Just concern yourself with the fare. I must say, it smells good."

As if hearing his introduction, a thin boy of about fourteen slipped into the galley and made directly for the dishes. His head bowed, he loaded his arms with plates and cups and disappeared through the door.

Was that respect or fear of Tate? Maybe his threat to throw her into the sea if she failed was not an idle one. Shaking away the thought, she smiled. "The tea and coffee are brewed. Your food will be ready at any moment. Then, I shall see to the crew. They do eat in shifts, right?"

"Yes. Twenty at a time. Four shifts. Make sure there's always hot water for the men to drink. They will want a beverage and I won't have them seeking rum until after the sun fades. Captain Stuart's cabin is there." Tate pointed a muscular arm down the long corridor to a door. "The boy will take his food. If he is there, he will be either asleep or working and will not appreciate being disturbed. We shall see at breakfast how you have done. If the captain is not pleased, I shall be forced to toss you to the sharks."

There was a gleam in his eye and Adriana laughed out loud. Tate seemed puzzled by the sound of it. She had to remember to be more careful in her manners and speech.

"Is that what truly happened to the last cook?"

Tate shrugged and turned away.

Fear rose again and she shoved it back. Death on land or death at sea? Well, she might have been the indulged daughter of a wealthy man and a spoiled only child before, but now she was a cook and would not fail. The old Adriana, courageous and full of confidence, would have served her well now. Adriana must try to summon her old self back.

Chapter Three

After the first full day, Adriana breathed a huge sigh of relief. Never had she cooked for quite so many in unfamiliar surroundings, aided by no one but the sweet soul who brought pails of water and the cabin boy. It was not an easy situation, but she was succeeding. Her confidence returned. Tate would not have to throw her overboard. Sometimes God smiled on your efforts and gave a helping hand to ease the way.

She would miss the fullness of the spring at home. The scents and bursting of green always wiped away the pervading desolation of winter. There had been so much joy in picking bouquets of colorful flowers from the meadow and placing them in vases all about the manor. Her life had been filled with so many pleasures until her perfect world had been shattered once, twice, and then once more. First, her mother had died, then her father. Then, her stepmother had sought her death with a vicious assault.

The days settled into a grueling routine of cooking and scouring pots, but Adriana found hard work enjoyable, even though the soft white skin of her hands was roughened, chapped from the constant chopping, peeling, and building up of the cook fire. There was no scented lotion to soothe them and, at night, when the small cuts and sores reminded her of her unglamorous lot, she tried not to wallow in pity. Three meals a day for so many kept her occupied, and the crew, delighted with the food, was very pleasant. Every night, the eye patch would come off and be wrapped around her hand lest she forget to replace it in the morning. She would rise before the sun, adjust the scarf about her hair and touch the edges with flour to ensure its grey color. There was a small canister of dark face paint in her bundle and she would mix it with some water and darken beneath her eyes, along the hollow of her cheeks and on each side of her mouth. The patch in place, she was again the old cook. Unless someone took time for careful inspection, the ministerings would be sufficient. She was careful to keep her head bowed most of the time.

The only thing she found disconcerting was the man who directed the ship. It was indeed the captain from the docks. Her heart nearly exploded inside her chest. It was as if he were a magnet and she but a pathetic piece of metal drawn in with not a bit of control. It was almost embarrassing, since she had never pursued a man. It had always been just the opposite. Now, when cooking, Adriana imagined carrying his breakfast to bed.

Captain Stuart.

Adriana Stuart.

She found herself sneaking onto the deck whenever there was a moment to spare. She wanted to see him. On the occasions when she was successful, her blood pumped so hard she thought her veins would burst.

Some days, she caught a glimpse of him and her insides would fill with light. It was not just that he was so handsome, which he was. Something about him stirred her soul. If time passed without seeing him, she felt bereft, but the cloud whooshed away if he appeared. He would smile at an errant comment from one of the men and his even, white teeth would stand in sharp contrast to his sun-darkened skin. And that mouth. She dreamed of having those lips on hers. What would they feel like? She had never really been kissed before—just an errant brush of her lips by a suitor being bold—but her imagination ran wild.

One morning up on deck, Captain Stuart was conversing with Tate, his legs wide apart, hands linked behind his back. He appeared so comfortable and relaxed and she had to squash a sudden urge to come up behind him, slip her arms under his, and lean her head between his shoulder blades.

She nearly laughed out loud wondering about his reaction to such an improper gesture from an old woman. He would most likely clear his throat and carefully move away from the creature that had certainly lost her wits. Ah, but it would be worth it. To feel the strength of his body and stroke the wisps of hair that escaped from the queue at his nape, if only for a moment. *You are a scandal*, she chided herself. *You should not even think such thoughts.*

She was careful lest someone catch her watching. What would be the excuse? She could say she was old, not dead? She appreciated a good-looking man? Of course, in the past Adriana had always had more than her share of suitors, but this man was so different. This one fueled desires she had never experienced. Last eve she had lain on her cot, picturing a life with this man. Captain Stuart. She did not even know his Christian name.

Fearful she would be caught staring, in the precious minutes she had to spare, she sought a secret place. She found she could just fit into a small space between two large crates on the lee side.

She was tucked away when the only other female aboard stepped into sight. Obviously a passenger, the woman was dressed for fancy tea and her nose was lifted high. So much for the bad luck of having a woman on board. She turned to one of the young men who was coiling a very long, thick rope.

"Get me some tea."

"I would, ma'am, but I cannot leave my work. After this, I must see to the mainsail. I am sorry."

"You most certainly are sorry. If I had but known how rude the men on this ship would be, I would never have agreed to this voyage. Well, I suppose I must see to everything myself." With that, she huffed away.

The young crewman screwed up his face in disbelief. He must have wondered where the female thought she was.

Adriana had been shocked. The woman had no notion how hard the crew worked, how long the hours and how difficult the tasks. This was not her young ladies' drawing room. It was a working ship. Which reminded Adriana that she was part of the crew as well and needed to tend to her own duties.

As dawn lightened the sky each morning with its glorious and vast array of colors, she boiled the water and carried steaming mugs up to the men working since the night before and those just rising to face the day. She prayed Captain Stuart would be walking along the rail, gazing at the sunrise, so she could but watch him. The crew greatly appreciated her thoughtfulness and, if he was not in evidence, she was still pleased to be able to take a few moments to breathe in the fresh morning air.

Daily, she was made aware that the ocean was a miracle in itself, stretching on for endless miles into an unknown infinity, shades of blue changing with each shift of light. The morning rays skimmed the surface and winked, beckoning one to enter and explore the darker patches. She was fascinated by the sheer vastness of it and wished her gaze could penetrate below the waves into the world that thrived there. The sea was calm some days, not so different from a river. It reminded her of the endless green carpet of the meadows at Beresford. The green beckoned there, too, only it did not whisper secrets. It was as it appeared and did not inspire caution. How strange that she was now far more secure skimming these unknown depths than the solid earth.

She kept to herself and her work, but occasionally at the evening meal, she managed to peer across the corridor at the formal dining table to catch a glimpse of the captain. It was the only time of day that he would be stationary and she could pretend he was there waiting for her to join him. His back was to the door, so he had no idea she gobbled him up with her eyes.

Tate and four passengers sat at the table with him: three men, all older, and the young woman seen earlier. Several times, Adriana could not help but notice the young woman stared at the captain with unabashed desire, although unless she spoke to him, he directed his conversation to the men. She thought the woman extremely unattractive. It was not that her features were uneven, except she had no chin. Or that she was overlarge. Her hair was thick and luxurious and a lovely shade of auburn, and her complexion was flawless. But there was a hardness about the mouth that suggested some unpleasantness, a haughtiness. An occasional smile might soften her features, but it was conspicuously absent. One of the other men addressed her as Melanie when asking her to pass the salt.

"I cannot even get a cup of tea," she whined. "The service on this ship is not what I am accustomed to." There was no response.

Perhaps the woman's father—the gray haired man across the table from her—was taking her to Virginia in hopes of finding her a husband. There was a similarity in their features, although he was corpulent and his clothes too tight. His fat cheeks puffed out when he looked at her and a deep sadness filled the depths of his eyes. Adriana could tell he loved her, but he had no liking for her. It was obvious in the tone of his voice and he never sat beside her. It must be very disappointing for the man to have such a child. The other two men appeared to be business associates and kept to themselves, saying little and attracting less notice.

When Adriana had the opportunity to bring food to the table, which was rare since the cabin boy did much of that, she forced herself to keep her eyes from Captain Stuart. It was like trying not to look at the dazzling sun on a warm summer day. She felt the heat and had to resist basking in its warmth. Earlier, he had brushed past her in the corridor as she made her way to the deck. At that moment, she thought she could surely die and be content. Where he touched her arm, the skin burned, branded.

They had been at sea for several days when the captain finally appeared in the galley. Suddenly, he was there, towering over her. Adriana gasped and tried very hard to maintain her composure looking at that hard, muscular chest. Her heart pounded so hard beneath her breast, she was certain it was audible. She coughed to cover the sound.

"Are you well?" he inquired.

"Quite well, thank you, sir."

"I am Robert Stuart. We have not officially been introduced. Suffice it to say I am pleased to have you aboard my ship. The men have worked harder and are happier with your food in their bellies."

"Thank you, Captain." Robert. His name was Robert. She raised her eyes and tried to hold his gaze, but the piercing blue was unnerving. Penetrating blue, deeper than an ocean and more enticing. He was so damnably good looking, with broad shoulders and a lean waist. The soft, white silk shirt was open at the collar, in sharp contrast to the tanned skin beneath. She had to remember to draw in a breath. His legs were long and he moved with the rolling gait of an experienced seaman. She, on the other hand, could not stand so easily against the ships constant motion.

Mary longed to pull the patch from her eye so she could see him more clearly. She wanted to absorb every nuance of his appearance so it could be recalled at will. Instead, the hot blush shot into her face. She dipped her head so he would not read her thoughts. It was no wonder that spoiled Melanie focused on him.

Robert now stared down at her. He appeared puzzled and she worried her masquerade was not convincing enough, but it was too late for self-recrimination. She would have to stay calm and continue on until it was clear the charade was uncovered. For now, she was content they were at sea and headed west to a new land.

He cleared his throat. "Well, I just wanted to welcome you and let you know that, so far, your work has seemed most satisfactory." And he was gone.

It took several moments to recover. She feared her

heart had leaped from the confines of her chest and she would have to search for it among the pots and pans. Then, she smiled so broadly she feared her face would split apart. She placed her hands over her chest and twirled about. On the third spin she banged into a wooden barrel against the wall. Has there ever been a more desirable man? *Back to work before you simply melt into the planks and sink into the sea with your silly fantasies.*

Chapter Four

Several weeks had passed and the weather had grown steadily colder at night. When Adriana went to her bed one night there was a warm woolen blanket laid at the edge. It was an ugly brownish-grey, and quite coarse to the touch, but she was delighted with the gift. Only months before, it would have been thought of as rags. Today, it was as wonderful as the finest brocade coverlet and would work well to keep the chill night air at bay. *I suppose I did not appreciate what I had. Such a spoiled and selfish girl.*

After breakfast the next morning, Captain Stuart appeared in the galley. "Morning, Mary."

Adriana could only swallow. Something seemed to have gotten caught in her throat—probably her heart that had jumped out the other day.

"Just thought I would let you know bad weather is coming. And storms. Not unexpected this time of year and much worse in the winter months. The clouds on the morning horizon were tinged with red. Not a great sign. The sea is an unpredictable mistress and her whims make fools of us mortal men. Have you ever been on a crossing like this?"

Regaining composure, she smiled. "Why?" she inquired nervously.

"I have been told you are comfortable at sea."

He had inquired? "I think I have adjusted. I like ships. The ocean is like…" She quickly closed her mouth, unwilling to give away a total lack of experience.

"Well, I hope you keep liking it when the waves rise and the ride is rough. If you have a weak stomach, I suggest you eat light until we pass into calmer waters. But something tells me you shall be quite all right. You do not strike me as a delicate type, like those society ladies." He pursed his lips. Had his eyes rolled upwards as if he'd been referring to the willful Melanie? Adriana kept her imagined delight inside.

"Oh, Captain, I do believe you might be surprised by the grit in some of those ladies of society."

"Perhaps. Meanwhile, if the ship is being tossed about, there can be no cooking fires. Dried beef and biscuits will have to do. I fear the men will grumble since they have been spoiled by the fare you have been preparing for them. But fires are not worth the risk. You had best be securing the galley."

"I thank you for the warning. Would you like some coffee or tea? I have made it fresh." *Please linger so I can look at you.*

"Thank you, but I must be at my work."

Adriana made an effort to concentrate on securing loose utensils and pots, more than a bit nervous about the impending threat of bad weather. She ached for someone to comfort and hold her, to stroke her hair and offer reassurance. But there was no one. Her thoughts drifted to Robert Stuart and she wondered what it would feel like to be in his arms. She conjured the image of a storm-tossed ship riding the waves, snug and safe in his bed, surrounded by his warm protection.

The upheaval came a day later. Adriana had mentally steeled herself, but was still woefully unprepared for the vengeance and fury of the ocean as it tormented their vessel. The screaming of the wooden boards convinced her the ship would be devoured by the heartless water at any moment. There was little air in the galley and many times her gorge rose. When she tried moving about, she was thrown against an unyielding wooden wall. With no cooking to occupy her, she spent most of the time clinging to the cot desperately trying to feel better. She was ill and terrified and sure she should never recover. The odors from the galley combined with the smell of old wood filled her nostrils, making the idea of nourishment a torment not to be endured. She decided she would have to feel better in order to die.

She berated herself for the foolish decision to come aboard this ship in the first place and for being a coward and running from a secure home. To prevent screaming her fears aloud she bit down on her lip, drawing blood. She was convinced they would all end in a cold, wet grave in the dark depths of the ocean. The dread extended to her captain and Tate, and the sweet, young cabin boy who helped every day. The thought she would never lay her eyes on Robert Stuart again only added to her misery. Why had she been such a fool? Death by gunshot would be preferable to this slow and painful torture.

Adriana had been the indulged and adored daughter of Daniel and Catherine Booth and her childhood had been full of laughter and joy. Daniel was an earl and had all the privileges of that rank, including wealth. To the horror of his own father, who believed those of title should never earn money, Daniel had decided to become a physician. But Daniel had held to his dream and had a

27

healthy and fulfilling practice. When, at a masquerade ball, Catherine had lowered her mask, they fell madly in love. The couple was married within weeks.

One terrible day, when Adriana was twelve, her mother was thrown from a horse. Daniel, even with all his skill, could not save his beloved wife. Her neck had been broken and he was bereft. He blamed himself for his lack of ability, for letting her ride alone that fateful day and for letting her die while he stood by helpless. Devastated, he gave up his practice and retreated to the library and the comfort of brandy. As terrible as the loss of her mother was for Adriana, she strengthened her resolve to support her father. There was a hole in her chest only a mother's love could fill, but she populated it with warm memories and the fierce love for her sire.

After three years, Adriana decided it was time for her father to rejoin life. She dressed in her finest gown and took extra care with the coiffure. When she appeared downstairs, Daniel had smiled in appreciation.

"Then, perhaps you can take pity on me. I have no escort this evening and I fear I have not the courage to attend the party alone. Perhaps I should just go back to my room and go to bed."

"No escort? Surely that is not possible." Daniel Booth was no fool and recognized when he was being manipulated. "Maybe someone will appear at the last moment?"

"Would you?"

"Adriana, I am no mood for parties."

"Papa, it has been three years. Come with me tonight. Please."

He shook his head. "If I do not agree, you will be relentless. Am I correct?"

"I fear it is the truth. So, you may as well just acquiesce now."

"You test me."

"I love you, Papa."

But that had marked the beginning of the end.

The recollection drifted and then faded and Ariana longed to go on deck, instead of dying here, alone, but she would be a hindrance to the men who fought to save them all. So, instead, she hid her head under the blanket on her cot and cried away her terror.

One morning four interminable days later, Adriana awoke with a start, sensing something odd. It was calm—as if the maelstrom was something she had conjured from an overactive imagination. She sat up quickly and moved into the cooking area. The familiar buckets of water waited. She hurried, knowing the men would be anxious for decent food after fighting the watery demons. She wanted to kiss the planks and each of the crew who had so valiantly brought them through safely. A hearty and delicious breakfast would have to suffice to show her gratitude.

A large pig had been butchered, cut into manageable portions, soaked in brine, and brought to the galley in several barrels. Silently thanking the dear soul who did that work, Adriana set to the task at hand. Soon, the delicious aroma of roasting pig filled the area and the hard work and fears of the past few days were forgotten as the crew ate heartily. Even the passengers seemed to have recovered from the storm's abuse, although Melanie still appeared rather wan.

Adriana was proud of herself for surviving. She had embarked on this adventure with little more than indistinct plans, some bravado, and the experience of spending much of her childhood in the kitchen with the cook. She smiled to herself at the thought. If only Cassie could see her now, Adriana imagined she would be stunned and, hopefully, amazed. She might also be aghast at a young lady with Adriana's breeding working like a common kitchen wench. Of course, Adriana was *head* kitchen wench.

After breakfast, Adriana cleaned the galley and laid out carrots and potatoes for the next meal. She organized her preparations and actually had some time to spare. It would not be amiss to bring Robert some fresh coffee. It would offer an opportunity to be near him if he was in his cabin. The thought lurched her heart up into her throat. She longed to feast her eyes on him, especially after days believing she would never again have the chance.

She entered without knocking, as Tate instructed, and caught her breath. Robert grinned as he pulled up his breeches and fastened them. "Sorry, Mary, but I can only assume you have seen a naked man before." He laughed out loud at her stunned expression. "Or mayhap I am mistaken—in which case, I apologize for shocking you."

He pulled on his white shirt and tied back his thick, black hair. He gratefully took the steaming mug of coffee from her hand and strode from the cabin. Adriana leaned back against the closed door and tried to breathe normally. She could not push the picture of his partially naked body from her vision and the hot blush burned her face. He was magnificent. She moved about the cabin, occupying her thoughts with other things. She prayed she had not stared too obviously and giggled at the hope she had not drooled on herself.

Robert Stuart was obviously very tidy. The cabin was efficiently designed and clean. A bookshelf lined one wall and a raised bed dominated the seaward side. The middle of the cabin boasted a desk bolted to the floor. Its surface was covered in charts, a straight edge, and a log book. Quills stood ready next to the inkwell. She picked up a vest that had fallen to the floor from the back of a chair and brought it to her nose as if to inhale the man himself, then gently stroked the leather as it was set back in place. She touched and straightened this and that, looking over her shoulder lest he return without warning. How would she explain herself? What excuse would there be? *I will only take another moment,* she promised herself.

A creaking of boards outside the door froze her. Then, the footsteps passed by. Knowing she risked discovery made it all the more exciting. It was like peering into his secret place and the thought was thrilling. She stepped to the bed and stared at it boldly. Scandalous thoughts came unbidden. He was there, unclothed and she was kissing him. The gown she wore slipped to the ground and he reached for her. She chastised herself for this turn of mind. Ladies did not think such things. Virgin ladies at that.

Chapter Five

The voyage had been longer and parts of it rougher than Adriana had anticipated, but all too soon it was nearing an end. When the sea was calm, it lent a wonderful feeling of freedom. In fact, she had grown quite content, which was unexpected in such unfamiliar surroundings, to say nothing of the constant hard work. There was much to be said for the security of knowing an assassin did not hold you in her sights. Even the terror of the storms had been nearly forgotten.

Tate came into the galley one evening and kept her entertained for several hours with his stories of Virginia, their intended destination. She shared his enthusiasm for the land and the people and anticipated with pleasure the thought of a new life and a new home.

Tate's voice was soothing and her thoughts drifted. She would be pleased to feel dry land beneath her feet again, but she would miss…? What? Or was it who? Adriana forced herself to admit she would miss the chance encounters with Robert Stuart. She believed the voyage had rattled her senses, since how could she possibly miss someone she had barely spoken to? Perhaps Tate would relate something about him that would feed her imagination and dreams. She dare not ask. It would seem suspicious if an old woman desired personal information about the captain.

Suddenly, she was ashamed at the turn of her thoughts. It was downright scandalous. What would her father have said? Her stepmother? Not that she ever did anything correctly in the eyes of Sarah Jane Booth.

Sarah Jane had been at the party that fateful night and had immediately attached herself to Daniel's side. She seemed warm and sympathetic, with a joy for living masking a secret longing for wealthier circumstances. Sarah Jane was beautiful in a cold way, oozing charm. And knowing that Daniel Booth was a very wealthy man, to say nothing of the title he bore, made him even more attractive. She was ever present after that night, stopping by to bring small gifts, offer to help with the household, making herself virtually indispensable. Adriana was thrilled, for she believed Sarah Jane would lift him from his misery and aid his return to life. The woman had finally had her way into their lives and, after a year, she and Daniel were married.

The changes began after merely a week of wedded bliss. Sarah Jane became more demanding, using snappish, impatient tones. Money flowed out in a constant stream for the acquiring of new gowns, new decorations, and furnishings for the manor.

As time passed, Adriana changed as well. Childish prettiness had stepped aside, replaced by the bloom of womanhood. Her figure softened and curved and her small breasts swelled into fullness. Her green eyes seemed to take on a mystical quality, accentuated by the long, dark eyelashes unchanged from youth. Fair skin, long, silky blonde hair and high cheekbones completed the vision of loveliness.

As her beauty grew, so did Sarah Jane's resentment. She constantly reminded Adriana of some fault, insulting her clothing, the color of her hair, anything she could name. She countermanded any request Adriana made of the servants and shushed her when she tried to speak.

One day six months ago, Daniel Booth had suddenly died. The doctor said it was a broken heart, which infuriated Sarah Jane no end. She worried the gossips would have a field day with that little tidbit. Humiliation fed her rage and discontent.

Adriana went to the funeral, her sadness tempered with a feeling of peace. She tried not to notice Sarah Jane's histrionics and demand for sympathy, as such a display had been expected from the woman. Adriana would miss her father, but she was convinced her parents were finally reunited and her father was free from the shrew he had married. It was a comforting thought. She went patiently though the rituals, graciously accepting condolences from her father's many friends and grateful patients, even as Sarah Jane sobbed into a lace-edged handkerchief.

Adriana felt vaguely sorry for her stepmother and patiently ignored the glares and looks of disgust from the other woman. She hoped Sarah Jane would be happy with her inheritance and, perhaps, soon have another husband to torment.

When the time came for the reading of the will, however, both women were in for a shock. Daniel Booth had left the bulk of his estate to his daughter, including the manor, which had been in their family for centuries. Sarah Jane was to receive a monthly stipend, but needed to vacate the family home in a month's time.

There was one small provision, however, and when it was read, Adriana felt a prickling of dread at the back of her neck and down her spine.

Paul Kernley, the family solicitor, knew what was coming, since he had drafted the document, but even so, the color drained from his face. "In the event of my beloved daughter, Adriana's death, the estate will revert to my wife, Sarah Jane, as there are no other family members." Kernley shook his head.

Oh, Father, have you signed my death warrant? Adriana chided herself for her silly turn of thoughts. Sarah Jane Booth was not a kind or charitable woman, but it was a major leap to characterize her as a murderess. And yet, when Adriana glanced over at the woman, a sickening grin had twisted Sarah Jane's lips. Then, very quietly, Sarah Jane rose from her chair and moved to Adriana. Leaning down, she whispered, "Take good care, for I intend to see you in hell." Then, she had turned away and left the house.

Adriana was upset by the veiled threat, but when Sarah Jane did not reappear after several days, Adriana put it out of her mind.

A week later, Jason Hadley returned after a long absence. And she was actually happy to see him.

Chapter Six

Adriana realized Tate had asked a question and it brought her back to the present. "I am sorry. What was that?"

"I asked what you were thinking, since you obviously were not listening."

Adriana was embarrassed. "I suppose I was wondering what life will be like for me in Virginia."

"Well, I would not worry. With your skills, you can easily find employment in the colonies. There are so many opportunities these days. Or perhaps, sign on with another vessel for the return."

"And why, if I chose to return, would I not be welcome aboard this ship?"

"Aye, you would if this vessel was returning. But she is to be in port for a while. The captain has decided to stay ashore for a time. He has property and business to attend."

"Oh, I see. Well, what of you, then? What will you do?"

"I am the captain's man. I go where he needs me. Even if that means staying on land until he is ready to set sail again."

"Will you not miss the sea? You strike me as a man who is happiest when the ocean is his home."

"Too true. The captain, I know, is reluctant as well, but he has no choice. His mother is depending on him. The message he received was clear. He was to return as soon as possible. A shame really." He paused. "You know, I imagine the captain might have use for a cook himself at his home. He has made mention, more than once, that good food is lacking there. In fact, I think I should suggest that to him."

"Thank you. If he is interested, I shall think on it. How long until we reach land?"

"Three days should see us home."

"Then, I suppose it is safe to confess to you now that I have never been aboard an ocean going vessel before." Adriana dropped her head in shame.

Tate laughed out loud. "Do you think me stupid, woman? Did you imagine you would fool me?"

She blushed and looked up at him. "Are you angry?"

His voice was soft when he replied. "Angry? Nay." He patted his rounded belly. "'Tis the best food I have eaten aboard ship ever. Why should I be upset with you? You kept your word, never complained. Even Captain Stuart was happy. Truth be told, you made me look good in his eyes and I appreciate it."

"Thank you. Thank you for everything."

He rose to leave, but hesitated. "Mary, I have one question. I know 'tis not my business, but my curiosity has gotten the better of me. Why did you need to get aboard the ship?"

She dared not tell the truth, but she hated to lie to this man who had been nothing but kind. "It seems I was indirectly responsible for another's unhappiness. I cannot say more. Only, I have committed no crime and am not guilty of anything. I hope that answers your question."

"Not really, but as I imagine it is all you will tell me, it will have to suffice."

Chapter Seven

The dawn would bring their destination. A new beginning. Adriana had taken whatever spare time she had the last few days to walk on deck and squint toward the horizon. First the land was a smudge of gray. Hours later, it defined itself into an irregular shape, then later formed into what could clearly be seen as shoreline.

She had come through this voyage with her identity intact. Having funds would allow making her own choices. It was amusing to think that, should the need arise, she could always find work as a cook on another ship. Or at the home of Robert Stuart. She had visions of looking at him with a lovesick gaze throughout every meal. No. Mary was to be left behind, aboard this ship, replaced by a proper lady. Continuing to work for Robert would mean seeing him every day, but it was not the solution. She had deceived him, but she knew in her heart a man like the captain would not take kindly to that, no matter her reasons for the masquerade. And could he ever not see Mary when he looked at her, even if she doffed her disguise? In fact, he could be returning to a wife and family for all she knew, although she thought Tate might have mentioned it if that were the case. No, the situation was untenable. Once they made landfall, she would have to make her own way, without him.

Adriana became aware of a presence. She turned and looked into the deep blue of Robert's eyes. A moment of panic was spent fearing he might have heard her thoughts. "Captain," she breathed.

"Tate indicated this will be your first visit to the colonies. I can only assume you would value a place to go and employment to sustain you. My home is desperately in need of someone who can prepare a decent meal." He stared at her for a moment, waiting.

She was unable to respond immediately. The very presence of him stole the words from her tongue. She could only manage a weak smile. Clearly satisfied, he nodded and turned on his heel.

Robert Stuart was obviously a man used to getting what he wanted. In his own thoughts, he would be convinced she had no other options and her hesitation had been based on something other than a negative response.

In fact, his confidence was irritating, especially because he had the power to render her without speech. She wished to walk right up to him and pull off the scarf, scrub her face clean and flash jewels in his handsome face. That might remove some of his arrogance. It would have given her some small measure of satisfaction to wipe that all-knowing smile away.

Darkness fell and the ship's crew settled for the last night as Adriana put the galley to order. Several of the crewman along with Tate, had gone to the captain's cabin after dinner to share a grog or two and celebrate the successful conclusion of their journey. She had overheard them say the ship made good time crossing and word was the cargo would reap handsome profits for all concerned.

The men's laughter floated down the corridor as she finished stowing away the remaining pots and pans. She couldn't fathom the reason why, but she would miss the cramped, stuffy corner with its lumpy cot. She moved to the bed and withdrew the bundle secured there since before they sailed. It seemed a lifetime ago.

She opened it and shook out the velvet dress. It was wrinkled, but not as badly as she had anticipated. Underneath was a soft undergarment that felt like heaven. She reverently stroked the soft silk. It struck her how much she had missed such finery. With any luck, she would be able to return to being a well-bred eighteen-year-old soon.

Then a thought struck. Was more deception needed? The colonies were filled with so many seeking a new life and what they hoped would be endless opportunities. It was quite possible no one would give heed to yet another, especially with her newest created history. She would present herself as a widow, whose husband was lost on the voyage across. It was a common occurrence to succumb to the rigors and travails of the trip. It would be more easily acceptable than a woman traveling across the sea unaccompanied which would no doubt arouse suspicion.

Over these last weeks, it had not been easy to feel clean at the end of the day. The kitchen odors permeated every single thing. They even adhered to her skin. With so little water available for other than cooking, it was difficult to do anything but the most minimum of bathing. The two times she had been able to wash her hair during the voyage, she had reveled in the clean feel before streaking it with flour to create its 'grey' appearance. Tonight, it would be washed again so it would be fresh when she left the ship, even still concealed with the scarf until she was safely away from the vessel.

Adriana had managed to set aside a bucket of water for that very purpose and now dragged it to a corner of the pantry. It would not serve for prying eyes or a casual visitor to the galley to see her without the masquerade. But all was quiet and there was little chance anyone would seek her out this late.

Adriana remembered when getting the servants to bring hot bath water would create a battle of wills. The staff already bore the brunt of Sarah Jane's cruelty and, rather than upset them further, Adriana did chores for herself. The servants were very unhappy with this turn of events since it was their job to care for the one they considered their true mistress. Unfortunately, they'd feared Sarah Jane's wrath more. Cassie, the cook, and the kitchen became her sanctuary. Cassie spent endless hours teaching her to plan meals and prepare them, choosing the right ingredients and spices.

Adriana had hesitated to appeal to her father, knowing he still pined for his beloved late wife and was oblivious to the horrible treatment his current wife doled out to all. His comfort was only found in the bottom of a bottle. Adriana was desolate for him and for herself, but there was no real solution. She felt responsible for his marriage to Sarah Jane.

Now, sitting on the edge of her cot, she untied the wrap around her hair and the heavy plait fell down to just above her hips. She unbraided it, anxious to have it return to the bright golden locks beneath the filth. The mass was like a heavy cloak. A bit of soap and water would see it softened and sweet smelling.

Adriana reached into her bundle, questing fingers finding a comb and the small bar of jasmine scented soap used so sparingly during the trip. She scrubbed her skin and her scalp until the lingering smell of cooking diminished. Once on shore, bars and bars of soap with lovely, heady fragrances would be the first purchase. But just now, the thought of putting on the old, dirty dress was more than she could bear. *I will put on the silk chemise and the velvet dress, if only for a few moments. It is already so late, no one will know.*

The rich fabric felt so incredibly luxurious next to her skin, Adriana delighted in the touch of it. She hugged herself with pure joy and twirled about in the confined space, then laughed out loud when she toppled back onto the cot. She desperately wanted to feel like a woman and a lady for a few more precious moments.

She stood and wondered if she actually dared to go on deck. The risk could be too great. If she were seen... She tilted her head toward the ceiling, attentive to any sound. All was still and quiet. The men had long ago left the captain's cabin. Adriana guessed they had consumed a great deal of rum and sought the comfort of their beds.

She eased out from the galley. From there she could see the captain's cabin. He, too, must be fast asleep. No light squeezed beneath the door. Adriana's heart ached to see him. Tomorrow they would depart from this vessel and he would be lost to her.

If she could but see him one last time and perhaps, if he was asleep, touch his cheek or lay a soft kiss on his brow. She quivered with excitement at the thought.

Heart pounding furiously, Adriana slipped down the narrow corridor toward his cabin. There was no movement anywhere. She edged closer. The guard on deck would be watching the shore from the port side and would have no cause to come below. The others would be deeply asleep, the intoxicating spirits seeing to that.

The night air filtered down the hallway. It was cool and filled with the scent of the sea and promises. She summoned all of her courage and gingerly tested the doorknob. The door opened.

He lay on the bed, his features even more handsome in repose.

She slipped inside the cabin, easing the portal closed and drank in the sight of him. A groan and Adriana jumped. He rolled over, took a deep breath and was again asleep.

Chapter Eight

Robert knew he had drunk too much. He usually refrained from socializing with his crew, except at the evening meals, but their goal was in sight and it might prove to be his last voyage for a while. It depended so much on how his estates fared since the death of his father. If he had to stay in Virginia for an extended period, he knew he would long for the freedom and beauty the water provided.

Robert had fallen in love with the ocean as soon as he was old enough to read about voyages and walk along the shore. He had seen the vessels come and go and dreamed of jumping aboard and exploring the world, seeking adventures in strange lands. At the age of eighteen, to the displeasure of his parents—they had hoped he would take over management of their considerable estates—he made up his mind.

He booked passage as an apprentice on one of the larger vessels. After five years of voyages to England and back, Robert felt ready. The captain had agreed. "You know what you need to know for now. The rest will come as you feel the forces of nature, loving you or conspiring to kill you. You will have to deal with issues and cargo and a hundred things I have probably left out of my teaching. But you will learn. Hopefully, the hard lessons are behind you."

The captain of the Windstar was retiring and Robert was not to be denied. He set about hiring a crew and was lucky enough to acquire Tate, who gave him not only a wealth of experience, but also a great friendship. The adventures had gone successfully thus far.

This night, Robert had invited the senior members of the crew to share a grog or two and reminisce. Most had been with him since the beginning. He knew his men thought of him as a good captain. He saw to their needs and pushed them to their limits when necessary. He also treated them fairly and gave them a just share of the profits.

As much as he loved the sea, at twenty-eight he must give her up for a short while. Other responsibilities loomed larger, most notably his obligation to his parents.

It was the middle of the night, but the rum and his thoughts refused to let him rest. Some fresh air would help clear his head. He attempted to sit up and reach for his breeches, but they eluded him. His feet had barely touched the floor when he saw her. He was quite sure it was his imagination—a state induced by the liquid spirits, no doubt. But, if this was the kind of dream it created, he must be sure to acquire more.

She stood silhouetted in the soft moonlight streaming in through the porthole. Glowing pale, creamy skin, and thick, luxuriant hair flowing behind her like dark manteaux. She wore a dark dress with a low, square neckline that enhanced the upward swell of full breasts. His eyes moved down to a slim waist, then back up. The light of the moon surrounded her, giving an otherworldly appearance and he was certain an angel had come from heaven to alight on the wooden planks of his ship. Or perhaps it was a mermaid who had managed to shed her tail for this night to torment mankind with glorious beauty.

Robert shook his head to clear it, then stopped, realizing this might make the vision disappear. He sat there, transfixed. She was pressed tight against the wall. He beckoned with one finger bidding her come closer, but she didn't move.

Then, suddenly, she sighed. The soft sound struck him like a physical blow and he jerked back as if he had been struck. She appeared so real, but this could not be possible. The only women aboard were the old cook and Cabot's daughter, Melanie. And the latter was certainly no beauty, not even in the most flattering light. The cook was well into her later years. So this magic could only have been conjured by his alcohol-soaked imagination. The silvery moonlight danced on her translucent skin and kissed those tresses with tiny flickering lights and the angel summoned him without so much as a spoken word.

He devoutly wished he had not had so much to drink, for his head refused to yield any logical thought. He gave up trying to think rationally and, instead, pulled himself up from the mattress. At first his feet refused to support his weight. He forced them to a semblance of stability, but when he moved, they threatened to buckle. Robert stopped halfway to the angel. He'd heard stories of people wandering the deserts of Africa for days becoming so disoriented they saw mirages—blessed lifesaving oases. Surely, that's what he was seeing here. If he went closer, would she disappear as those visions did?

No way to know unless he tried. Robert took two more tottering steps. Only a few inches separated him from the spirit woman. A wonderful flowery scent filled his nostrils. What was that? Jasmine perhaps. Surely a mirage didn't smell sweet and clean and wonderful. He lifted a hand. And touched her face. When she didn't melt like smoke and disappear, he pulled her tight against him. Oh God. Had there ever been a better sensation?

She made a sound that seemed to catch in her throat: a combination of terror and excitement. She stiffened momentarily and then molded her body against him. Now, Robert was completely confused and unsure. His dream had warm flesh and blood. His manhood rose in response. Who was he to question the fates? He would see this dream to its natural conclusion. After all, what harm could come from making love to a vision? The scent of her was so beguiling, so irresistible, it made his head spin like a child's top and brought memories of sultry summer nights and secret lands. He was intoxicated and it was more than mere rum.

Chapter Nine

When he sat up and moved toward her, Adriana was terrified. She had taken a risk and lost and now her secret was exposed. But his gaze was unfocused as he moved closer and the expression on his face was one of disbelief. She shrugged inwardly. Since he must know the truth, and she was so desperate to touch him, just once, she decided to throw all caution to the wind. It was possible the strong drink would toy with his memory, was it not?

Adriana's heart threatened to burst from the excitement of how this was unfolding. A fantasy come true. It was almost more than she could bear. She could smell the rum and hoped he would be too inebriated to remember this encounter. This was a risky game she played. Her very life was at stake. Did she dare give in to her desire to be in his arms, if only for this brief time? And what would he recall come morning light? A female? If he did remember holding a young woman for a few moments, perhaps he would think she was Melanie Cabot. After all, their hair was similar. The cabin was dark and he was drunk. What more harm could come of this?

On impulse, she turned and looked into his eyes. He was watching her as if she was the strangest thing he had ever seen. She decided to toy with him. Perhaps some of his earlier arrogance would be quelled.

"Good evening, Captain," she murmured. The throaty sound of her voice seemed to mesmerize him. This was madness, but it no longer mattered. She wanted to feel his lips. She had never really kissed a man on the lips.

Brazenly, she wrapped yearning arms around his neck, entwining her fingers in his hair and pulling his mouth down. As their lips touched, a tingling erupted in the pit of her stomach, then spread out in undulating waves—like the storm that had tossed the ship a few days ago. Robert's kiss deepened. His tongue probed between her parted lips as if tasting the sweetness of her mouth. Adriana's entire body caught fire. She pressed against him, desperate for she knew not what.

She stroked his chest, the touch igniting her in a way that was new and frightening and exciting, all at once. He ran his cheek against her neck, the rough beard scraping her skin and sending shivers of delight through her body. He placed his lips at the base of her throat, nipping, tasting. His fingers slid under her bodice to cup a breast beneath the soft velvet of her dress. She gasped as he brushed the sensitive tip, then kissed him more deeply, demanding. It felt as if she had been dying of thirst all of her life and he was a river. Then, suddenly, she was in his arms and being carried to the bed. It was now or never. The last chance to change her mind. But like a starving person placed before a platter of meat, Adriana could no more deny herself a delicious taste of Robert Stuart than the starving man could deny his own ravenous appetite.

Placing her on the bed, he moved to lie next to her. His fiery kisses traced a path along her throat and moved to her breasts. Adriana gasped as he released her from the confines of the dress and his tongue toyed with first one pink peak and then the other. She was exposed to him and her senses were reeling. His hands were everywhere, touching, sampling, loving. She knew she must stop this madness. She had only wanted to be near him, but this was beyond all reason. She had to get away, before it was too late. Her reputation would be destroyed if this continued.

She pushed against him, attempting to rise from the bed, but merely succeeded in slipping her leg between his. The hardness of him probed her thigh. Panic rose.

"Captain," she whispered. "Please. You must stop." She had to stay his hands from burning her flesh and weakening her resolve. "Captain, they will hear us. Someone will come in."

His knee shifted and her legs parted. His hands stroked the skin of her inner thigh. His hand felt rough—and incredibly arousing—against her soft flesh. She desperately wanted more. That place between her legs heated until she felt she would die if the flame remained unquenched. His fingers artfully moved higher, seeking the treasure at her core. They slipped into the slick wetness of her womanhood. She nearly cried out at these incredible new feelings. He worked his fingers until he touched the small, hard nub at the entrance. Adriana held her breath as she was driven to a height she had not known existed. Then, he stopped all movement of his hands. Sensations didn't ebb. Rather they grew, turned into an ache. Adriana feared she would simply dissolve in agony.

All at once, his mouth was on her breasts, teasing, licking, the hard peaks rising and begging for more. His tongue painted a scorching, oh-so-slow walk down to her belly and, oh God, lower, into the juncture between her thighs. His lips sucked at the hard center of her being until she could bear no more. Suddenly, the world exploded in white-hot flames and she buried her head against his shoulder, shuddering with the force of the blast escaping through every nerve ending, every pore.

Before she could regain her senses, he had thrust himself inside her, his hard, throbbing rod replacing his tongue. She bit down on her fist as pain burst within her. Miraculously, the pain subsided and was replaced by an incredible warmth that spread unbelievable pleasure throughout her body. He drove deep within her, at first slowly and then faster. She moved with him, her body arching into his. Her legs, of their own volition, wrapped themselves around his waist, pulling him deeper yet. Adriana felt herself rising higher and higher on the wings of ecstasy. When she thought she had reached the pinnacle, he took her higher still. The passion thundered within her and she felt herself burst into a thousand pieces as he stiffened and moaned his own sated pleasure.

Robert sagged against her, his head moving to her ear. "My Lord, wench, never have I had a dream like you. If this is what lays in store for me in my bed, I think I shall never again awaken." He smiled and pulled her tight against him. A thousand thoughts chased themselves through her brain, but she could muster none of regret. If she never saw this man again, she would never be sorry she had let him make love to her. The truth was she had fallen for him from the first encounter when she glimpsed him at the dock. And now, at least, she would have this memory forever, come what may. He had drifted off to sleep, his breathing soft and even and she relaxed against him, hoping for just a few moments more. But her body betrayed her and she joined him in sleep until Adriana heard his voice, husky again with his need, drawing her to wakefulness.

"'Tis nearly dawn, wench, but I am not prepared to let this go quite yet. There are some questions I suppose I should ask…"

His sentence floated unfinished as his hands explored her body again. She held to him tightly, feeling the heat of him, returning his passion measure for measure. This was foolishness, but he awoke in her feelings she never even dreamed could be. She vibrated with his touch, throbbed with his caresses. She never wanted to leave this man and yet, she must fly as soon as she could.

Gently, he made love to her again, and she had never felt more loved or beautiful and she reveled in it.

He settled back into sleep, nuzzling her neck and throwing his leg possessively across her thighs. She inhaled the masculine smell of him, savoring it, and stared at his handsome features.

Suddenly, she realized she could see him clearly. It was dawn and the sky was becoming brighter with each passing second. She had to fly from here. Her mind raced. She had to somehow get back to the galley before she was discovered.

She eased away from him careful not to joggle the bed. He moaned and reached for her. "Captain, I must go for a moment. I will return, I promise. Sleep now."

He settled back smiling and she slipped from the bed, grabbed her dress and chemise, and pulled them on as she moved to the cabin door. Looking back at him for a brief, sad moment, she eased into the corridor and headed to the galley. A noise froze her in her tracks and her pulse raced. Was that the creaking of a door? Had someone seen her leaving the captain's cabin? How would she explain? Chastising herself for taking such a risk, she could do nothing now but plead for mercy. But she saw no one. Still, panic moved her forward and, her eyes open wide, she scanned left and right. Nothing. Just her imagination.

With a huge sigh of relief, she scurried into the galley.

Chapter Ten

Robert opened his eyes slowly; a pounding headache driving in the reminder of how much he had imbibed the night before. He rose very carefully, valiantly trying to keep his head from rolling off his shoulders and across the floor. He wished the ship would cease its violent spinning.

He squinted at the narrow porthole and wondered why God hated him. An overcast sky would have been a blessing since the bright light threatened to blow his eyes from their sockets.

Before his thoughts could clear, Tate threw open the cabin door and strode in. Damn the man. He had had as much to drink last night, but looked none the worse for wear.

"Fine Captain you are. We're about to make port and you be still abed. And ye look like hell. Shame on ya. And why are you grinning like some fool?"

Robert leaned back against his bed, remembering bits of the night and the sweet smell of lavender or was it jasmine? He looked down at the scene of his pleasure and realization hit him like a physical blow. He stared at the sheets, the stain of red in vivid relief against the white. He jumped forward, naked, as if he had been scorched, mouth agape.

Tate stood by the door looking as if his captain had gone utterly mad.

"Where is she? I wish to see her. And then you can damn well explain how you spirited her aboard."

"Who, Captain? Who are you talking about?" Tate looked totally perplexed.

"Stop playing games with me, man. I am not in the mood. Did you know she was a virgin?"

"Captain, Tate said very slowly. as if talking to a child with limited understanding. "We all had a healthy draught of rum last eve, but I would not have thought it enough to bring on visions."

Robert was prepared to continue raving at Tate when he thought better of it. Perhaps it was not Tate's doing. The other man did honestly look confused. Robert scrubbed at his cheeks and immediately regretted the action. "I thought I dreamed her. But look." Robert pointed to the bloodstain on the sheets. "And her scent lingers. Can you not smell it, man?"

Scent. That was always the part that stayed with him. The way a woman smelled. So like flowers, yet so unique. Rebecca always left behind a remembrance of roses. It haunted him so much that he could not bear the odor for years after they parted. Rebecca—beguiling and beautiful and treacherous.

Robert had met her after he landed in England one autumn. He had gone to a party and there she was. Thick blonde hair, sparkling blue eyes, and a figure that would drive any man mad. He was instantly taken with her and it seemed she felt the same. He began courting her and each encounter found him more and more devoted. He was so much younger then, and so naïve. His friends had warned him often that she was but a butterfly, ever seeking the sweetest blossom, never satisfied with the bounty of one. He was crazed with desire for her and turned deaf ears. He thought them envious or ignorant of the true woman only he could see. Lavishing her with expensive gifts, he would have done anything to see her smile at him. The smile of a pit viper, but he was so unaware then.

Finally, one night, he gathered his courage and took her out on the balcony during a dinner party. He had gone down on one knee and pleaded with her to be his bride. She had laughed at him. And she continued to laugh as she went in and rejoined the others, leaving him bereft and humiliated. The sounds of their amusement trailed behind as he sneaked away.

He had sailed as soon as he could gather his crew and load some cargo. And Robert swore no woman would ever have the opportunity to make light of his feelings ever again.

Robert had heard Rebecca was a duchess now. He had also heard that she fueled the gossips with her ever-scandalous exploits and the constant cuckolding of her husband had made the man a laughing stock. Better him than me, Robert thought, knowing it was uncharitable, but relieved all the same.

What of his promise to himself? And yet, here he was, railing about finding yet another one who had left him, albeit under far different circumstances.

Tate stared openmouthed for a moment, then lifted his gaze to the captain's. "There are only two women on this ship, since no one else has come nor gone. If a woman had rowed out to meet us and boarded, it would certainly not have gone unnoticed.

"So that leaves but two possible women: the

passenger, Miss Melanie, and Mary, the old cook. Did you really bed Miss Melanie? Her father will see you married to her. What were you thinking, Captain?"

"It could not have been Melanie. It was another, I tell you. Young and beautiful and the most desirable woman I have ever encountered. Search the ship. Perhaps she stowed away. I must find her."

***

Adriana had barely made it back to her cot when the ship lurched. The men called out as they set the anchor. She hurriedly removed the velvet gown and slipped on the old, torn cotton dress. She quickly braided her hair and secured it around her head with the scarf, carefully applying flour to the wisps that stuck out. She smeared some of the dark makeup to her cheeks and under her eyes and reached for the eye patch she had discarded the previous eve.

Old Mary, the cook, was again in the galley. Grabbing her cloak, she checked that the bags of coins and jewels where she had hidden them in the lining were untouched and folded the garment on itself. Finally, she was finished and stopped to catch her breath. She almost screamed out loud as Tate came up behind her.

"Morning, Mary. If you could see there's coffee and tea enough to go around, that will suffice for this morning." And he was gone, but her pounding pulse reminded her of the risk she had taken the night before.

She set about starting the fire and boiling the water. She wondered how much time would elapse before she could escape. She very much feared the captain would awaken and realize her presence had been more than just a rum-induced vision after all. What of her disguise? He must know. Would he betray her? Send word back to England? Of course not. Why? The way he touched her could only be love.

She remembered the feel of his hands and his mouth as they explored the secrets of her body. She recalled the passion and the myriad feelings that had flooded her. She exhaled. It cannot be that love can happen so quickly. Or could it? Perhaps she was just taken with the fact that he was the captain and very handsome. No, that was not it. It was the man himself.

Everything about him captivated her. He had enough power as a landowner to provide protection from Sarah Jane if he chose. Adriana had been so careful and had made the crossing with none the wiser. But now, her deception could prove more than just passage to the colonies. It could be the beginning of a completely different future than she had imagined. She would reveal herself and he would sweep her into his arms, wouldn't he? Or had she seemed a common whore? That must be how she appeared last night. She had shamelessly fallen into his bed. Why had she been so brazen, so stupid?

Adriana poured coffee and tea into pots and took them across the corridor to the tables. She fussed with spoons to stop her thoughts of last night, but they were relentless. He would certainly question her motives. Would he ever be able to trust her? If not, then what? She had already given him the most precious gifts. If he rejected her, she was ruined. What man would have her now that she was spoiled? She would be resigned to living alone or finding some man to marry who could forgive her indiscretion. The prospects were not appealing.

Perhaps, though, during their night of rapture he had

fallen in love with her, too. Maybe he secretly knew the truth and merely waited for her to reveal herself. He would appear at any moment and proclaim his undying affection and beg her to be his wife. They would be married and life would be perfect.

She was completely lost in her future as Adriana Stuart with several children at her skirts when Tate interrupted. "Come on, Mary. The men are waiting in the boat to take you ashore. Then they shall see you safely to the captain's house."

Before she could protest, Tate had retrieved her bundle and cloak from her cot. He guided her up onto the deck and helped lower her into the waiting boat. There was no time to think before she was on dry land and being led to an old carriage.

The dray jerked away from the pier and the ship, purportedly taking Adriana to her new home. This was not the vision she had hoped to fulfill. The ship grew smaller as the conveyance moved out into the countryside. What now? Of course! He must know she wanted no one to know her identity so this would allow discretion. Brilliant! He is seeing that I am escorted to his home and it is there he plans to declare himself.

Adriana wondered where Robert was this morning. She had not caught sight of him and thought he might have been delayed with some business to do with the vessel. If that was the case, she must change from her old dress and reappear as Adriana. I cannot have him proposing to me looking like something dragged out of the dustbin.

Chapter Eleven

The ride to the Stuart home was breathtaking. Adriana sat there, awed by the brilliant green of the rolling hills, the endless fields of vibrant green tobacco swaying in the breeze and the gracious homes set back from the road, like jewels scattered carefully about in some great plan. The air was sweet and full of sunlight and the warmth replaced the months of sea air in her lungs. She inhaled deeply, the breath of the new world filling her with delicious promises. She sat on the edge of the seat, fearful of missing even the smallest detail of this new home. She drank it in like someone dying of thirst and relished each sip. So many possibilities. So much beauty in this place. The sun pierced the ceiling of thick leaves from the trees that stretched like a canopy above the road. So peaceful.

First, however, she must discover the intentions of Robert Stuart. Unanswered questions tormented and held her back from fully languishing in the magnificence of the scenery. What now? Would he declare himself? How could he not? But what must he think? When should she shed her disguise and reveal herself? He must already know the truth. No answers presented and in too short a time, they had turned into a long drive lined with tall oaks. What was obviously the Stuart home sprawled majestically ahead. It was almost entirely made of brick, with wooden columns in the Greek style. Tucked behind the pillars, a veranda stretched the length of the structure. The house dominated the terrain, surrounded by flat fields covered in ripening crops that bespoke a rich harvest.

The red brick of the house was complemented by myriad colors. It was the time between spring and summer and the flowers burst into a glorious array, competing for the prize of most beautiful. Some of trees were heavy with blooms and the heady scents mingled with the sun and the grasses and all thoughts of cramped quarters and fearsome storms abated. Adriana thought this rivaled even the home she had left behind in England and she quelled a brief spasm of homesickness. Now was not the time. She had assessments and decisions to make.

Apparently, the captain had left the ship ahead of her, since he now stood on the veranda with Mr. Cabot and his daughter, Melanie. Behind Robert, an older woman had placed her hand on his shoulder as if for moral support. His mother, no doubt. She was a clearly a formidable woman, although the top of her head barely reached Robert's shoulder. Her stance was strong and her defense of her son unquestionable. The two men were locked in what appeared to be a heated argument and the older woman looked furious. Robert kept shaking his head until, finally, Mr. Cabot turned to descend the steps. Melanie meekly followed her sire, looking not in the least repentant. There was no doubt she was the cause of this agitated debate.

As Adriana's carriage pulled up, Cabot called back over his shoulder and Adriana could finally make out his words. "This is not finished. You have ruined my daughter and you will make it right." Pulling Melanie behind him, he mounted his own carriage.

"If I had, I would. But I did not, sir." Robert's angry voice rang out as the vehicle pulled away, but Adriana heard an underlying uncertainty in his tone that caused her to wonder. What had that been about? Ruined? Realization dawned like a jolt to the stomach. Melanie had claimed to be the woman with Robert the night before. Adriana recalled the sound as she'd left his quarters. It had been made by slippers rushing into a hiding spot. Melanie had been there, had seen her leave and was using it to now cry out for justice for herself.

"Hah." Adriana gave an unladylike snort.

Justice, or more likely a husband, since she would have no way to gain one otherwise. Well, certainly Robert remembers it was I. Now, I must come forward and declare myself.

Before the carriage had fully stopped, Robert was pulling open the door. "Mary, tell me. Tell me you saw her."

Adriana was caught by surprise. "What? Her?" This was not possible. He was asking her about... herself. Could he actually be so blind? So stupid?

"There was a woman aboard the ship last night. Did you see her? She was lovely, with long golden hair and— and not Melanie Cabot. Did you see her?"

Was he making sport with her? Could he truly not see through her disguise? Well, two could play, if truly it was a game. "A woman? I am a woman."

Robert smiled. "Well, of course, you are. But I meant another. Younger. Not that I mean you are old. I just meant..."

"I understand your meaning." Adriana tried valiantly not to pluck out one of his eyes. Of course, then he could borrow her patch. "Are you sure? Perhaps you had a bit of seasickness or... I have heard that a bit too

61

much grog can make one see things." Could he not hear the sarcasm dripping in her tone?

"I have been told as much," he growled. "But I did not imagine this, no matter what opinions I receive on the matter. She was real and flesh and blood and I shall not rest until I find her." He spun on his heel and headed into the house, his body rigid with anger and obvious frustration.

Adriana could not fathom it. He did not recognize her in the slightest. It was unbelievable. She had given her most precious gift to man who did not have not have any idea who she was. There were no words... Fury raged inside and she had trouble drawing breath. This was unbelievable!

Robert had disappeared into the house and it was left to the driver to aid her in leaving the carriage. A manservant stepped forward. "I am Jamison and I am to show you to the kitchen." The man's tone was very businesslike. Adriana was so angry, she barely noticed his words. Without thinking, she obediently followed him through the grand foyer, from which majestically rose a winding staircase. The walls were alive with dancing rainbows cast by the intricate crystal chandelier. The oak floors shone from hours of polishing and portraits of what she assumed to be family members were elegantly displayed along the stairway wall.

Beyond, a corridor led into a pantry, with a formal dining room to the right, dominated by an impressive cherry wood table glowing in the morning sun. There were place settings for two, but enough seating for at least a dozen more. The high-backed chairs were covered in beautifully hand-embroidered fabric and the sideboard gleamed with silver serving pieces. The cream colored wallpaper was flocked with a deep red velvet that echoed the velvet in the heavy drapes.

The style was quite different, but the richness and elegance of the appointments and furnishings made Adriana homesick for the gracious life she had left. She briefly closed her eyes and took a deep breath. She was humiliated. How could this have happened? Robert should be begging for her hand in marriage. All she could think now was to escape as quickly as possible.

Suddenly, a terrible thought struck her. If the captain continued in his insistence on a beautiful young stowaway, her deception might be uncovered and everything she had done to maintain anonymity would have been for naught.

She followed Jamison outside and across a tiny courtyard fragrant with herbs and into the impressive kitchens. Once inside, the butler seemed to vanish into thin air and a large woman stepped up to her. Her smile was warm, her expression kind and welcoming.

"Hello, Miss Mary. I am Hazel and I sees to the running of this place. I was told to expect you and heard praises about your talents as a cook."

The larger woman with the dark skin had huge, soft brown eyes that seemed to miss nothing. Hazel's smile was contagious and Adriana grinned in return. But something came into the other woman's narrowed gaze that made Adriana wonder what she was thinking. It was almost as though the woman could see right through the disguise and into her very soul.

"Thank you," was all Adriana could manage, so many thoughts fighting for attention in her head.

"Come on, I will shows you around the house."

Hazel led the way back into the courtyard and into the main building. They walked past the dining room and to the library across the corridor. Clearly a man's space, it reminded her of her father's, with walls of books and comfortable leather furniture. Further down the hall, in sharp contrast, the morning room showed obvious evidence of a woman's touch. The room was a study in sunshine. A delicate bookshelf on one wall was dressed with tiny porcelain figurines. The sofa was small and covered in a pale yellow and cream striped silk that matched the two chairs on either side. A vase of fat roses fairly dominated the small writing desk.

"Where do the roses come from?" Adriana asked. "They are so beautiful."

"We have a man who can coax violets out of the snow."

"You are teasing me."

"Just a little. But it do be amazing what the man can get to grow. And Miss Elizabeth sees to it he is happy here so no one can ever draw him away. In fact, the Stuarts are good to all of us." The loyalty communicated by remark was undeniable.

They moved on to the drawing room and then circled back around to the pantry. A back stairway led up to the third floor and Adriana followed Hazel up and across a hallway to a small, neat bedroom with a bed and dresser. It was a welcoming space and Adriana smiled. The servants were indeed treated well here and that spoke volumes to the Stuarts' character.

Adriana set her bundle and cloak on the bed, then turned back to see Hazel blocking the door, her arms akimbo. "I needs to know you have the right intentions. I loves this family and I will not see anything happen here."

Adriana was completely caught off guard. "I beg your pardon?"

"You is not who you says. You do not fool me. You are not old. I bets you are not even blind in the one eye."

Adriana had no idea how to respond. After a moment of hesitation, she decided the truth was the best choice. She laughed out loud, then shook her head. "I deluded a crew of eighty and the captain for many months. How is it I could not fool you for even a short time?"

Hazel smiled. "Menfolk is nowhere near as smart as they thinks."

"I beg you not to reveal the truth. My life would be at risk."

Hazel narrowed her eyes. "Tell me the whole story and I might keep your secret. The truth now."

Adriana dropped her shoulders in resignation. "I had to flee from my home. My stepmother shot me and wanted me dead so she can inherit my father's estate. I had no other way to ensure I would not be killed. So I disguised myself and played the cook on board the captain's ship. No one making inquiries would think that I was the old lady Mary. No one, but you, that is."

Hazel raised her eyebrows. Clearly, she thought this to be a farfetched lie to cover some deeper secret. Adriana read her reaction and moved closer to the black woman. She reached up and pulled down the left shoulder of her dress, revealing the small round scar, the skin pink and twisted. Hazel nodded solemnly.

"I could use your help in making good my escape. I had no idea the captain would offer me employment and bring me here from the ship. I need to find my way back to town."

"And then what?"

"I will rid myself of this masquerade. I can take care of myself. I just had to make sure no one knew I was coming to the colonies." It was a relief to be able to speak of her dilemma.

Hazel was quiet for a time, then nodded. "I will helps you since I believes you. But we needs to get you out of this place without being seen. It is several miles to the town of Williamsburg, but when you walk it, you can change your clothes on the way, in the woods, and get there as the young woman you are."

"Thank you. I will owe you a debt of gratitude forever. Just point me in the correct direction and I will disappear." Adriana reached for her sack. "But what will you tell the captain?"

"I will tell him you already gots a better offer. I will say I tried to convince you to stay, but you had your mind all made up."

"You are an angel," Adriana exclaimed.

"Wait here a few minutes, then come back to the kitchen. I will sees you have some food to takes with you. All you has to do is just head east and you will gets to Williamsburg."

Chapter Twelve

Robert had barely had time to hug his mother in greeting when the Cabots had drawn up to the house. His mother had been shocked by the vehemence of Cabot's demands and when the man stormed away, his very unappealing daughter in tow, Elizabeth had turned to Robert for explanation.

They had gone into the comfortable and well-appointed drawing room where she had ordered tea before turning expectantly to her son. "Welcome home officially, Robert. I really am delighted you are here. However, I see you have been followed by some controversy. Would you care to explain?"

"I missed you, too, Mother." He grinned at her. Sobering, he said, "I am so sorry about Father. I will miss him."

"I, too. You have no idea the hole in my heart since he has gone. But it was partly a blessing. Toward the end he was in so much pain. He fought long and hard. The doctor said the disease could not be stopped." She took a breath, clearly holding back the desire to break down into tears. After a moment, she regained control of her emotions. "But we can talk of it later. For now, I fear a more immediate problem requires resolution. Would you care to share the details?"

Leslie Hachtel

"Have I a choice?" he asked with a raised eyebrow.

His mother gave him a look he recalled from his earliest memories. It spoke of the dangers of crossing the line into disobedience. She had never had to do more than direct narrowed eyes at him and he was willing to do whatever it took to lessen that ire. Naught had changed, even though he was fully grown.

"I will tell you what I know."

After he gave his mother the details of that night, as clearly as he could recall, she sat back and shook her head. "So, you bedded a virgin and you have no idea as to her identity, but Miss Cabot swears it was she and her father is now demanding you make an honest woman of her."

"In simplest terms."

"And you are sure it was not Miss Cabot."

"Mother, I was drunk, not blind."

"Be kind."

"I thought I was."

"Well, truth be told, she is an unusually unappealing example of womanhood. I am not sure why she seems so. She is pretty enough I suppose, but there is something… well, repellent about her."

"Now, mother, be kind," he admonished her.

"I thought I was." She laughed with him. Growing more serious, she continued. "So, who do you imagine to be the other woman?"

"I would give anything to know. But, apparently, she does not exist."

"There must be an explanation. There were no other women aboard?"

"Just the old cook."

"Old cook? Who is she?"

68

"Mary. I brought her home. I mean, I hired her on as a cook here. She is most gifted with limited supplies, so I can only imagine she will shine when given the abundance of our pantry."

"She is an old woman? How old?"

"I know not. But old."

"Could there have been a stowaway?"

"Tate says no. They searched the ship."

"Well, you had the proof on your sheets that the woman was not just a dream, so there must be a rational explanation. I am hoping, for your sake, you were not blinded by drink. It does happen. But for now, it appears Mr. Cabot has left us no means to dispute his claim. If you despoiled his daughter, you have no choice but to be a gentleman and make it right. And of course, there is always the possibility she carries your child."

"Dear God, there must be some way out of this. I do not think I can face a life with that miserable shrew."

"So she is mean as well?"

"As an angry bull. You should have heard the way she spoke to my crew—as if they were each one her personal servant."

"Then you have my sympathy. You know you must agree to marry her if she is with child."

"You cannot truly expect me to wed the woman?"

"I cannot expect you to do anything but act with honor. You must see to your responsibilities and face the consequences of your actions. It may not be pleasant, but it is necessary."

"There must be another way."

"If she is not *enceinte*, perhaps they will find some other arrangement acceptable. Or it could be that she will decide to tell the truth."

Robert shot her a look of disbelief. "I would love to believe that, but I fear she has her sights set on a life of comfort and she intends for me to provide it."

"Or," she continued, "perhaps we can come to an equitable negotiation."

"Equitable negotiation? I need to be free of these charges. And free of the virago who makes them."

"Find the woman you believe shared your bed. If she exists and will come forward, you will be unburdened from any obligation to the Cabots. That is the only way."

Chapter Thirteen

Adriana was startled into wakefulness. It took a minute to get her bearings and remember where she was. The hotel room was light and clean and did not sway. All so different from the Windstar. She lay back on the soft pillows, luxuriating in freshly laundered sheets.

She had sneaked out of the Stuart house and run across the grounds into the surrounding woods. She thought/hoped she had escaped unseen. She walked east and came upon a fast running creek in a small clearing. She had rested beside it, the tall trees surrounding her and bestowing shade. The eye patch was not needed any more. Neither was the flour and dark makeup. She had scrubbed her face clean in the cold water. Then, she had retrieved the comb and untangled her hair, shaking out the remaining flour that had turned the rich honey colored tresses around her face to grey. She re-braided the luxurious mass then changed into her velvet dress and slippers. Finally, Mary the old crone was transformed into Adriana, the young lady newly arrived in the colonies.

It couldn't be hard to find a proper inn and secure a room. Familiarizing herself with the town would be an adventure, she thought, swallowing the nagging trepidations. She would be strong. And she would never again think of Robert Stuart who had shared with her a night of magic and then failed to even recognize her. How could she have been so attracted to one so… so…? Well, she would wipe him from her memory and that would be the end of it.

She arrived in Williamsburg in the late afternoon, the shadows cloaking the wood and brick buildings as if to hide their secrets. The frenzy of activity was contagious and Adriana, although tired from her walk and nervous to be in a new place with nothing familiar, could not help but be caught up in the excitement. There was so much bustle in the streets here, no one paid heed to a young woman window-shopping as she walked along.

Adriana passed a milliner and a dress shop and what looked to be a nice hotel, which she approached. Across the street, a small, white clapboard building bore a sign in front: George Peyton, Attorney-at-Law. Tomorrow, she would gain some new clothes and visit the lawyer, but for now, she was exhausted and hungry. Hazel had supplied some biscuits and dried beef, but she had finished that a while ago, understanding what she had been told about Hazel's lack of skill in the kitchen. Now she was famished.

Entering the hotel, she walked to the desk to ask for a room for the next few nights and whether there was a restaurant close by. The clerk eyed her with a trace of suspicion, but took her money and held out a room key. He also directed her to the adjoining café.

Adriana smiled, took the key, then headed toward the beckoning aromas of food. It was nice to be served and the food, although simple fare, was delicious. Sated, she went to her room. There was a soft, welcoming bed with white linen and fresh air blowing gently through the open windows.

Exhausted, Adriana pulled off her dress and sank into the sheets, her thoughts straying to muscular arms and demanding lips before drifting into sleep.

Chapter Fourteen

"What do you mean, she had a better offer?" Robert's bellow of rage echoed throughout the quiet house.

"I does not know, Mister Robert. That was all she said. And she was gone. That is all she said," Hazel repeated. It was clear his tempers did not intimidate her in the slightest.

"Dammit. She was a good cook. And never complained. We desperately need a cook. You have many talents, Hazel, but you never did learn the value of proper food preparation. I was certain she would wish to stay. She said nothing to me about another opportunity. It makes no sense."

"I is sorry, sir."

"It is certainly not your fault. I am the one who is sorry. I have had a rough day and I am taking it out on you.

"Never mind. We will manage." Hazel left the room and Robert wondered why Mary's leaving had elicited his ire.

Feeling bereft rather than merely angry, he had to admit he liked the old woman, enjoyed her presence, and would miss her. Not that he had spent much time with her on the ship. There had been too many other things that demanded his attention. And that elusive wench! Who was she? He had to find her.

What about Cabot's demands? They were more pressing at the moment. No matter what the other man had declared, there was no question in Robert's mind that it was not Melanie he had made love to. It could not have been the mean-spirited shrew who had responded to him with such passion. He had seen her evil streak, in the way she dealt with the crew, and how she had addressed her parent. No, it was not Melanie Cabot who had melted into his body as if it was a part of his own.

But where had the other woman come from? How had she gained access to the ship? It made no sense. Mary was old enough to be his grandmother. He would never mistake her for the soft, yielding beauty whose hair floated to her hips and whose supple skin had carried the exotic fragrance of blossoms on the night air. He was certainly not so drunk he would have confused Melanie or an old woman with the magnificent creature he had held in is arms. It was not Melanie's unpleasant whine that had swirled in his head like a drug, driving him to the heights of passion. The mystery was making him insane. His mother was right. Without the other woman to refute the Cabots' claim, he would be left with the only explanation possible: that it was actually Melanie Cabot.

Cabot's petition that he make an honorable woman of his daughter was laughable. Ruined her for any other man? As if she could have other suitors. If he were to do the right thing, he would have to spend his married life inebriated in order to make love to his wife. There had to be another answer. God could not be so cruel as to saddle him with that bitch for the rest of his life.

Chapter Fifteen

Adriana sipped her hot coffee slowly, enjoying the time to think and decide her next move. It made sense to acquire an agent to represent her interests and keep her anonymous. The lawyer across the way seemed the obvious choice, so she decided to pay him a visit as soon as she had finished her breakfast and bought some new gowns. She must dress appropriately. She also needed to be seen as a woman of means, or no agent would trust her ability to acquire the things she needed, including a permanent place to live. And she needed to occupy her mind sufficiently to keep one Captain Robert Stuart from invading her thoughts. Damn the man. To him, their night together was a meaningless moment. Why, the fool did not even recognize her when they were face to face. Having feelings for him was ridiculous and she must not think of it. Her trip across the ocean had been merely a means of escaping danger. She had left nothing behind on the ship. Except, perhaps her heart. Hah, the fantasy of a child. Time to grow up and get about a new life.

She walked out of the restaurant and down the street to the dressmaker's shop. She tried on several sample gowns and was impressed with the cut and quality. Adriana was lured to the brighter colors, but a dark color would be more correct. Finally, dressed in a lovely black brocade with a square neckline, several similar dresses were ordered. Appearing as a widow would answer so many questions and stay the asking of others.

She crossed the dusty street to the office of the attorney, tapped on the door, then entered. It was sparse, with an old, scarred wooden desk and two plain chairs. "Is anyone here?"

Almost immediately, a small older man, lean, with the kind of face that spoke of intelligence, came from the back room.

"Can I help you?"

"Are you the lawyer?"

"Guilty as charged." He smiled at his little joke. "Sorry. Never can resist that."

"Nice to meet you. I am Adriana… Hadley." The name just came to her and she hoped Jason would have no objection to her use of it.

"George Peyton. Very nice to make your acquaintance, Miss Hadley." He motioned her to the only other chair in the room as he took his own behind the desk. "Now, what can I do for you? Tea, perhaps?"

"That would be lovely. And it is Mrs. Hadley." She smiled modestly, hoping to convey some vulnerability.

He hurried to the back and returned with two cups and a teapot. He poured the steaming liquid and pushed her cup toward her. "Sugar? Cream?"

"No, thank you. This is fine."

He waited while she took a sip of the hot liquid and returned the cup to her saucer.

"First," Adriana began, "let me caution you that this interview must be kept in the strictest confidence. It is most important."

"Let me assure you, Mrs. Hadley, the lawyer-client

relationship is a sacred one. I would not dream of breaking it." His voice seemed to convey a bit of trepidation, but he had a very sincere quality that made Adriana feel at ease.

"Excellent. Perhaps I am being overly cautious, but I feel better being careful."

"Mrs. Hadley, I absolutely understand. A woman in your position can fall prey to so much. Believe me, I will be here to offer whatever services and solace I may provide."

"Thank you. That makes me feel so much better."

"Now, how can I help?"

"I am newly bereaved and have no champion to see to my needs. My dear husband sickened on the voyage here and died and left me quite alone." She sniffed to convey her deep sadness and hoped she was convincing. She had thought out all the details and it all seemed simple enough. Death on the crossing was not an uncommon occurrence. The trip was long and hard and fraught with all manner of diseases and deprivations. "I will need to find a house, preferably just outside the city. It should be comfortable though not overly large. But, attractive. I should like to move in by the end of the week. This being Wednesday, that gives you three days."

"Mrs. Hadley, I am so sorry for your loss. This is certainly a very difficult time for you. However, I---"

"Mr. Peyton, if you cannot help me, I shall understand. But I do have adequate resources and you will be well paid for your services. So, can you help me or not?" This last was said with no rancor.

Peyton cleared his throat. "As a matter of fact, I believe I know just the house. Actually more of a cottage, really, but it should suit your needs. It is just outside the town limits and set back a bit from the road. It is brick and boasts a lovely fence. It was left in excellent condition when the owner and his wife had to move north. Let me make the necessary inquiries and I shall get back to you this afternoon. Where are you staying?"

"There is more."

"Of course."

"I shall need a gun. One not terribly large, but not a toy, either. Something I can learn to master quickly. And a horse. Later perhaps, a carriage and a driver. As for the horse, she should come from good stock and be well trained.

"I do not see any problem with your requirements."

Adriana rose from her chair and moved to the door. "Oh, please do not concern yourself with contacting me, Mr. Peyton. I have some errands to see to, so I shall return this afternoon. She turned to leave and abruptly stopped and turned back to him. "Good heavens, I nearly forgot." She walked back to his desk and dropped a sparkling emerald and diamond necklace on the desk. The stones were huge and sprayed the office with a rainbow of reflected sunlight. The piece was magnificent and clearly worth a fortune. Peyton's jaw dropped and Adriana smiled at him guilelessly. "I trust this will cover the necessary costs. Should you require more, you have only to ask."

Peyton looked at her with slightly narrowed eyes. Adriana laughed out loud. "I assure you the jewelry is mine. Have no fear you are dealing with a thief. Discretion is necessary for personal reasons, but I am not an unscrupulous woman."

"Of course not."

"Thank you, Mr. Peyton. Until this afternoon, then."

Chapter Sixteen

Adriana was perfused with a feeling of freedom. The breeze blew her new cloak out behind her like a dark bird taken flight. The sky was bright blue and clear and promised that the days of summer would stretch on. The proud chestnut mare ate up the rolling landscape, moving as though she had wings instead of hooves, leaving Adriana breathless and giddy. The horse was well built and had a sweet nature and she could run like the wind.

She had not felt so unburdened since… she could not remember the last time. Her thoughts had been plagued for so long with her own safety and then clouded with visions of a hard muscled chest and sweet kisses that permeated into her heart. Damn the man. A constant refrain. How could he not have realized her identity? Was she not pretty enough? Was her body not pleasing? Adriana had been so certain he was as in love as she and had to know her true identity.

She pulled her thoughts away from the source of her frustration and concentrated on her ride. She had named the mare Cinnamon and they had struck up an immediate bond. Now, Adriana had a lovely new home, a beautiful horse, and a gun to waylay miscreants.

A question gnawed at her. What if she had conceived a child with Robert? No, it was not possible. Certainly not after only one encounter. But, if it were possible, what then? He might deny it. Thank God she had thought to pose as a widow. At least her reputation would not end up tattered. Then again, perhaps her monthlies would come and all would be well. Nothing to do but wait and see.

The sun was dipping into the horizon, the panorama of magnificent colors breathtaking. She turned Cinnamon around and rode back, savoring the feel of the cooler air and the sweet fragrances of the earth. The wind kissed her cheeks and the hillsides blended with the sunset to create a palette filled with a riot of light and shadow.

She rode back slowly, rehearsing the story of her origins again and again. It was time to meet some people and become established in her new home. The more quickly she was accepted, the less likely she would ever be found out. If her stepmother could not find her, she could not harm her. As for her father's estate, well, she had sufficient resources to see her through. And Paul Kernley was back in England seeing to her holdings. She knew it would be unwise to send word to him unless it was utterly necessary, but it was still comforting to know he was there should she have need.

The next morning, she dressed carefully and walked the short distance into town to make some new friends. She had been here for two weeks and was anxious to dispel the loneliness. Adriana was not shy and had always found meeting new people came easily to her, so she assumed it would be the same here. It was such a lovely city, with whitewashed shops shoulder to shoulder whispering of their wares. It was so unlike the shouting and chaos of English marketplaces.

By the afternoon, though, Adriana was trying not to be discouraged by the reception she had received. She had smiled at several well-dressed women who looked right through her, as if she did not even exist. It was unnerving. The shopkeepers were just shy of rude. Desolate, she was walking back to her cottage when she nearly ran into a large man. Preoccupied by the town's coldness, she failed to notice him. Looking up into the man's eyes, his jawed dropped as recognition came. Tate.

"Truly? Miss Mary? Is it you. Hazel was right."

She could not stop herself from laughing. "Adriana," she corrected him.

"You are indeed both young and beautiful. How did I not see it before?"

"Good afternoon, Mr. Tate. It is good to see you again." She was nearing her home and she gestured to him. "Come in. I welcome the company of an old friend."

Tate stepped into the pretty little whitewashed brick house with the wooden roof. An overstuffed couch sat in front of a large fireplace and several other rooms branched off to either side.

"Sit down and I shall make us some tea."

He sat on the sofa, his bulk displacing the cushions as he sank into them. "You know, I suspected you were not an old hag, but I am still a bit shocked by your appearance."

"Why, Mr. Tate, I have never thought of myself as shocking to look at."

"Oh, no." He reddened visibly. "That is not what I meant, at all. Oh, you know what I meant."

"So, you figured out the truth behind my disguise. Does anyone else know?"

"It was Hazel who told me. She knew right off. Said your soft, unlined skin gave you away. And your walk. Hazel said it was as plain as the ---how did she put it? The

81

ugly nose on my face. That Hazel has a lot of sense for a woman. Can't cook, though."

"So, generally, women have no sense---is that correct?"

"You are doing it again. Teasing me. You know my meaning."

Adriana brought the tea and set it down on a low table in front of the couch.

"Do you have anything to go with it? I believe I have lost a bit of weight since we left the ship. I surely miss your good cooking."

"Why, I thank you, sir. So why have you come to visit and place flattery at my feet?" She was happy for the company. She had grown quite fond of this large man with his kind heart and gentle way. Some day she must inquire as to the origin of his scar. She retrieved some scones and cakes, and placed them before him. She could not restrain a grin as his eyes lit up at the sight. "How did you find me?" she inquired.

"That was easy. A lone woman newly arrived. A great beauty. Not too many choices. I was determined. I had two reasons to find you, both worthwhile. Still, I would not have recognized you unless I had been privy to your secret identity. I am so glad you nearly ran into me."

The thought of being so easy to locate sent a shiver down her spine. She had become complacent, believing herself anonymous in this new place. She would have to be more wary in the future.

Adriana sat across from him on a beautiful, tapestry covered chair and poured tea. She was about to hand him a cup when she noticed something odd. "Mr. Tate, have you taken to keeping mice in your clothing?"

His face was suddenly split with a wide grin. "Oh,

82

that. I nearly forgot." He reached into his coat and withdrew a small, wiggly, tawny haired puppy. It looked very tiny and vulnerable cradled in Tate's huge hand and Adriana immediately reached out to it.

"Oh, how precious," she cooed. "Why, he is the cutest thing I have ever seen. Is he yours?"

"Actually, she is a gift for you. And he's a she." Tate smiled as Adriana cuddled the puppy against her throat. Her warm tongue tickled as she kissed Adriana's neck vigorously.

"Well, it is clear she likes you."

"I love her. But I cannot accept such a present."

"Actually, you would be doing me a great favor by accepting her. The mother dog had a large litter and they need homes. When she grows, she can offer you protection. I know she will eat well under your care." He winked at her.

"Then that would be two, Mr. Tate."

"Two?"

"Favors. One for giving me a job so that I could come to the colonies and two, for this little angel." She kissed the pup on the top of the head and the dog's whole bottom section wiggled as she wagged her tiny tail. "I shall call her Blossom. After all, she looks like the small yellow flowers that grow wild around here. Do you like the name, Blossom?" The creature wagged her little tail again. Then, the pup sank into Adriana's lap and proceeded to fall asleep. Adriana stroked the soft fur, delighted with this new companion. She hesitated to admit how deeply lonely it had been.

"So, how do you find life in the colonies?"

"I am settling in. It will take time. I suppose I had greater expectations, but I am most comfortable here. I very much appreciate your visit and this little darling you brought." Adriana indicated the sleeping baggage in her lap.

"It was not just out of kindness."

Adriana looked at him and narrowed her eyes with suspicion. She waited and he squirmed under the directness of her gaze. "I—we—need your help."

"We? I am glad to give you aid if I can, since I owe you a debt of gratitude, but who is with you in your request?"

"Well, it is not as if anyone knows I have come. Except Hazel, of course. It was actually her idea. I told her everything but, as I said, she guessed the truth right away."

"Go on," she prodded.

"The captain is in trouble," he blurted out. "And only you can help him."

"Trouble?" He was in trouble? The thought almost made her laugh, but she stifled the inclination.

"It seems Miss Melanie is claiming she was the woman in his cabin that night and her father demands the captain marry her. She has gone so far as to claim she is with child. I say he was drunk, not blind."

Adriana already suspected this. She had seen the Cabots at the Stuarts when she first arrived and suspected Melanie was up to something. At the time, though, she had feared they were telling Robert of her masquerade as the cook. But Melanie actually had the audacity to try and pretend she was the woman who had visited Robert that last night. "Are you serious? She would not be so bold as to make such a claim. Why, it would shred her reputation."

Tate reddened. "Not if she could coerce him into marriage." He heaved a sigh. "I do not mean to embarrass you, Miss Adriana. Or bring up a topic I should not even be discussing. But I am certain you were the woman with the captain our last night out."

Adriana was aghast. How could he be certain, while the captain seemed to have no idea? This was infuriating.

"Please do not misunderstand. I have no desire to bring you discomfort, but seeing you now, it is obvious you were the woman he was with." Shaking his head, he raised his gaze to hers, pleading. "I cannot sit by and see Miss Cabot do this to the captain."

The truth was out. No more need for this deception. "Devious, scheming little thing, is she?" Adriana blew out a breath in disbelief. Then, she understood why Tate had come to her. "You want me to reveal myself and discredit her."

"Miss Mary, the Cabots promise to ruin the captain's reputation unless they can force him into a marriage with that woman. Hazel and I cannot sit by and allow that woman's schemes to come to fruition. If she had not pressed the matter, we would not have become involved. It seems Miss Melanie has her father convinced and that man will not rest until it is made right."

Adriana smiled. "I understand your loyalty to the captain. I admire it, in fact. But I have no such feelings for him. He did not even recognize me the next morning. In fact, when I arrived at his house, he had the audacity to question me as to the identity of his mystery woman. His stupidity has sealed his fate."

"You cannot mean that."

"I can and do. You found me. How could he not?"

Tate looked down at his lap, his thick fingers toying with each other. "I would not have suspected if Hazel had not told me. We thought we should let the two of you work it out, but obviously that was not the best choice. You cannot condemn him to a fate worse than death because he is not discerning."

"I can and will."

"Then, I shall have no choice but to tell the captain the truth and suffer his rage. He will not react kindly when he knows I have kept this from him."

Adriana took a deep breath. "So, what you are saying is he will find out either way, but if I come forward willingly, it will save you from retribution."

"Aye. And I would be forever in your debt."

Adriana looked down at the sweet pup in her lap and smiled. "I do this for you. As far as I am concerned, Captain Robert Stuart can go to the devil, but I owe you and will not sit by and see you blamed for his insensitivity."

"Thank you. From the bottom of me heart."

"I do have a concern, however. I took great pains to arrange my anonymity. If I reveal myself, who is to say word would not get back to my home in England? I would again be at risk."

"I honestly cannot imagine that happening. Word from here takes months to reach the other shores. Besides, how would the Cabots know the source of your threat? The Stuarts would not betray you and I think it is a leap to believe the Cabots would. If Melanie is discredited, she will be angry, but revenge on you would serve her naught."

"You have a point. I suppose I am as safe as I will ever be. And you are correct. The danger was on English soil, not here. So, how shall we reveal the truth?"

"The Cabots have been invited to dinner tomorrow night, presumably to reach some arrangement. If you could come and announce yourself, it would solve the problem."

Adriana thought for a moment. "On one condition."

"Anything."

"You are not to warn Robert I am coming. At least let me have the satisfaction of the advantage when I appear."

"You are entitled to that. I cannot express my gratitude. I will not tell the captain I found you."

"Until tomorrow, then."

He rose to go.

Adriana gently put the pup on the rug, where the tiny thing let out a little groan of comfort and slept on. "Thank you for my gift, although you clearly had an ulterior motive."

Tate grinned shamefacedly. "I had decided to bring her here to you, no matter your decision. But there is nothing like a small bundle of fur to tip the scales."

"You have no shame, Mr. Tate."

"And you, Miss Mary—Miss Adriana—are a woman above women." He took her small hands in his large, beefy one and squeezed. "Thank you."

Chapter Seventeen

Adriana had timed her arrival perfectly. What certainly must be the Cabot's carriage sat in front of the house, the driver lazing against the side of it. He paid no notice as Adriana descended from her own hired carriage with the help of her driver and went to the front door. It seemed so long ago since she first saw this place, dressed as an old woman. Tonight, she took great care to present quite a different appearance.

Her gown was of a deep burgundy brocade and squared at the neck to show her ample décolletage. Her hair had been swept into a mass of curls that spilled down her back like a glorious waterfall. Ruby earrings dangled from her ears. The overall effect, she hoped, would be dazzling. For tonight, she had shed the widow's masquerade. Those expected to be present this night would know it was a sham anyway once her true identity was revealed. It seemed forever since she had been able to dress to her own taste, without the protection of a disguise. And in dressing as she had, she was here to protect another, although she was convinced he did not deserve her charity.

The front door swung open and Tate stood there to greet her, a smile lighting his face. She had a moment to see into the parlor, where the Cabots and Robert's mother were speaking quietly. As she moved to step inside, Robert appeared at the top of the stairs. He audibly drew in his breath and nearly tumbled down the steps in his haste to descend. He shot Tate a questioning look, then looked back at Adriana. Tate merely grinned and disappeared toward the back of the house.

Robert swallowed what looked to be a cannonball, then spoke. "You are more beautiful than I remember. I was beginning to be convinced I had actually imagined you. Where did you go? Where have you been? I have searched high and low. Who are you? He shook his head, as if to dislodge mud. But here you are and I find I am completely nonplussed. You are magnificent." He led her toward the parlor and his mother stepped forward in greeting.

"And you, Captain, are an ass." Adriana hissed under her breath.

He looked at her, confused. "Why did you leave me without a word?"

"So many questions, Captain." The sound of her voice recalled what they had shared and she noticed with satisfaction his manhood began to rise. "Why, I was always directly under your nose, of course." She spoke for his ears alone. "So, make no mistake. I am here to return a favor, to save your sorry self, but tonight shall be the end of it. And too, it is because I have a sense of what is right and cannot see someone led astray if I can but prevent it."

He seemed so totally baffled by her conversation, she almost laughed out loud. "Your brain is more dense than even I imagined. I was the cook, Mary. On board your ship. Months at sea, I prepared your meals. You never even looked at me. And then, even when we spent the night together, you still saw nothing beneath the masquerade." She tried to conceal the resentment and anger, but it seeped out in her tone.

It clearly took him a moment before the pieces fit together. "That is not possible. You were Mary? The old cook?" He narrowed his eyes at her, obviously trying to picture her in the disguise. She could see it was a difficult transition for him, but it began to be clear. Realization came into his eyes. "How could I not have seen it? I am the most blind of men. How could I not have known?"

"I have asked myself the same question so many times."

"Can you forgive me?"

"No. But let us get through tonight so I may return to my life."

"I do not wish to let you go. You have haunted my dreams. The vision of you, that night, has been constantly occupying my thoughts. I have tried so hard to locate you."

"Obviously you did not expend too much effort since once more I have been so near the entire time. I care not for your wishes, Captain. Introduce me and we shall be done with it." Adriana swept past him and into the drawing room.

The Cabots turned as one. Mr. Cabot rose to greet the newcomer. His breath caught, his appreciation of her beauty reflected in his reaction. Melanie, on the other hand, looked as if she had just swallowed a lemon. Robert stepped up behind her.

"Mother, Mr. Cabot, Melanie, may I introduce M—."

"Adriana Hadley," she interrupted him.

Robert cleared his throat. "Yes, Miss Adriana Hadley. She was aboard my ship on the voyage from England." Robert then addressed the Cabots. "I do not believe either of you had the pleasure of her company since she kept to her cabin during the crossing."

A deathly quiet immediately settled on the room. It was broken by Elizabeth, who stepped forward to greet their newest guest. "So delighted to meet you, my dear. My son has spoken of little else since he arrived home."

Adriana smiled radiantly. "How kind. I am so pleased to meet you, as well. I regret that my business has kept me away so long. I am sure you are aware that your son and I fell in love. It was so sudden, you see, and I needed to make some arrangements when we landed. Now, however, we can go on with our plans together."

Cabot turned to Melanie, fury rising. "What is this?"

Melanie sputtered. "It is not true. I was the one. It was I, I tell you."

"The one?" Adriana asked. "What one? Robert, I am confused."

Robert swallowed. "It seems Miss Melanie claimed I bedded her aboard the ship on our last night out."

Adriana laughed out loud. "Do not be ridiculous. Forgive me for my boldness and candor, but that cannot be possible. I was with you that last night. And, unless your bed can accommodate three, we were alone. Forgive my reference to the indiscretion since we were without benefit of clergy." She looked at him with all the adoration she could muster for a convincing performance. She owed as much to Tate.

Adriana turned to Elizabeth. "I hope you do not think less of me, but I found your son to be irresistible. And, since we plan to wed as soon as possible, I am hoping you might be understanding as to our... impatience to be together."

"I understand about love, my dear. And you are both

young and the close quarters would certainly foster such… associations."

"I carry his babe," Melanie screeched.

Completely unruffled, Adriana spoke quietly, as if to a dull-witted child. "You know that is not true. I cannot comment on your state of virginity, my dear, but I can most certainly guarantee it was not lost with my Robert. I am sorry you find yourself so desperate as to try this deception, but the truth will come out. I have heard there are—places—an unwed mother can go until the child is born. Perhaps I could make some inquiries for you."

Melanie flushed bright red. "I will announce your secret," she fairly screamed.

"Secret?"

"You disguised yourself as the old cook. You were in hiding and I will expose you."

"She was the cook?" Cabot sputtered. Then he spun on Melanie. "How did you know this? That means you must have seen her with the captain." This last was said full of accusation.

He turned to Adriana. "I have no idea as to why you would feel the need to hide yourself, my dear, but that is your own affair. I am shocked that my offspring used this information to corrupt the truth." He again faced his daughter, whose jaw had snapped shut. "You made me threaten this man and make demands based on your fabrication, your lies."

Now, he spoke to Elizabeth. "Forgive me for any trouble I have caused. There is no joy in an ungracious and manipulating child. We shall take our leave and not bother you again."

"Father, I tell you it was I in his bed. How can you not believe me?" Melanie squealed.

Cabot took hold of her arm and pulled her out of the room. "This is not the end. I promise you," Melanie spat as her father yanked her out the front door.

The portal closed behind them, and sinking into a chair, Elizabeth sighed her relief. Then she turned to Adriana. "I cannot thank you enough, my dear, for joining us tonight and discrediting that deceitful woman."

"It seemed the honorable thing to do."

"So you were not a figment of my son's imagination. And you are so much lovelier than he described. Come, we shall have supper. There are many things I would like to know about you."

"It is very kind of you, but I cannot stay. I accomplished what I came here to do." Adriana turned to the door. Robert took hold of her arm. She glared down at the offending hand and he removed it. "Never touch me again," she hissed. Helplessly, he watched her as she strode out the front door.

Before the portal closed, Adriana heard Robert's mother. "Are you just going to let her go?"

"What can I do? She thinks I am an ass."

"Then, she is right. If you let her go, you are an ass."

Chapter Eighteen

Adriana hoped each day that Robert would appear and beg for mercy. She imagined him on one knee, tears streaming down his face, pleading for a crumb of her compassion. But she knew it was merely a fantasy. He was a selfish, hard-hearted man who was perfectly content to have spent one night of passion with her and then cast her off. Perhaps he did recognize her the next morning and merely decided to put her aside.

The night she appeared at his home, he made her heart nearly fly from her chest. She was sure his mother could hear it pounding. This just further stirred her anger. How dare he have this effect on her?

She had no doubt he was grateful for her intervention with Melanie, but she did not want him to come to her based on his gratitude. If only she could rid herself of these memories so easily.

Now, misery was truly seeping into her soul. She had many friends surrounding her all of her life and was unused to being so much on her own. As an only child, she might have been lonely for a brother or sister to confide in, but her childhood friend, Jason Hadley, was nearly always around. Since neither of them had any siblings, he was welcomed in their home as the brother she never had. When her mother died, it was Jason she turned to for succor.

He had gone away for three years and one day reappeared. Adriana was thrilled to see him at first.

"I have so missed you, Adriana. I am so sorry I could not attend your father's funeral. I loved and respected him very much. In fact, because of his influence I was thinking of pursuing medicine as a career." Jason's voice was choked with emotion. He had not changed much. He was still slightly short of stature, his complexion pale and his too wide set eyes made him owlish in appearance. A hooked nose dominated his face and his body was soft from lack of exercise. He was, however, still her Jason.

"Come in and I shall order tea. You must stay for dinner so we can catch up. Say you will, please."

Jason laughed out loud. "I would love to stay. I have been away too long already."

Jason became a constant in the Booth home. It had started wearing on Adriana, but she hesitated to appear rude. When other suitors would present themselves, he was in evidence, as if declaring her as his own. She was forced to take the other gentlemen aside and explain that Jason was merely an association from her past and she owed him for his loyalty.

"Just tell him to go," Cassie had counseled.

One morning, her maid, Martha, woke her just as the sun was beginning to stain the sky with pink and pale gray sunlight. It peered through the heavy draperies surrounding her bed as they were drawn apart, and Adriana immediately sat up, blinking away the sleep that lingered there.

"Is aught amiss? What time is it?"

"Very early, I know. But it seems you must get up and dress. Mr. Jason is downstairs and demanding to see you. He says it is urgent. He threatened to wake you himself if I did not hurry and come for you." Martha was older and had been with the family since Daniel, Adriana's father, was a mere lad. Her sweet countenance and grey hair, pulled back into a respectable bun, gave more the appearance of a doting grandmother than a servant. This morning, however, her features were tight with concern.

"Is he out of his mind? What could be so important that he must call nearly before the rising of the sun?" She was unsure whether to be angry or frightened.

Adriana threw on a heavy, red velvet robe against the chill of the morning and stepped into her slippers. Then, she hurried down the stairs and into the library, where Jason waited, clearly impatient.

"Jason? What is so pressing that it cannot wait until a decent hour?"

Jason turned and Adriana was taken aback by the look of naked fear in his eyes. "I came to warn you."

"Warn me? Of what?"

"I was at the waterfront and…"

"The waterfront? What business would take you there?"

"It matters not. What matters is what I heard and saw. Sarah Jane was talking to a large man about—taking care of some business. It was clear she was making arrangements to have someone killed."

"I do not understand."

"She gave him a purse and it was clear to me that the intended victim—was you, since she directed the man here. She was telling him that this would end her worries and there was another purse for him when the deed was done. I came as quickly as I could."

In her heart, Adriana had known since the reading of

the will that this was a possibility, but she had valiantly hoped she had been mistaken. "Jason Hadley, if this is your idea of humor…"

"Adriana, how can you say such a thing? How can you doubt me? And how could I make light of a threat to your life. I am afraid for you. But what I cannot conceive of is why. Why would she want you dead?"

Adriana took a deep breath. "If I die, she inherits the balance of my father's estate. She now has only a pittance, but if I—well, she would be very rich."

"Of course. I assumed it had to be about money, somehow. But you cannot ignore this threat. The man looked able to accomplish the task." Jason grew quiet for a moment. "You must go away where they cannot find you."

"Go away? From my home? It is unthinkable."

"Adriana, be sensible. There is a danger to your very life. You are no longer safe here. You must go. And I will go with you—to protect you. We should marry, of course. That way, I can see to your safety."

"Jason, this is happening so fast. I need some time."

"There is no time. I could not bear the thought of any harm coming to you. You must know how deeply I have come to love you, Adriana."

"Jason, I love you, too, but as a brother. As a friend. I cannot marry you. It would seem wrong. Do you understand?"

"Adriana… please. You could grow to love me as a husband. I feel it."

"Perhaps. But, for now I must decide what to do. Sarah Jane's actions have made me re-think things. I had no idea she would become an actual threat to my safety."

"I never liked her. She always seemed so—selfish.

Please reconsider my proposal. I know your heart could soften towards me."

"This is not the time." She held up her hand to forestall any reply and began pacing the floor. Finally, she turned back to him. "Go now and I shall send word to you later."

The bullet had shattered her shoulder soon after his departure. Jason was there when she woke up, acting the ever devoted suitor.

As the memory faded, she wondered if even Jason's company was preferable to this constant desolation.

She remembered having tea with the other ladies and talking of the latest fashions. Now, she ached for someone to choose gowns with her, helping her decide on which color and cut was the most flattering. She would love nothing better than to spend her days socializing, becoming part of the community. Her only comfort here was the puppy, and her horse, and Adriana sat in the sunlit parlor stroking the pup's soft fur as her thoughts became more disquieting.

What if she carried a babe? The thought sometimes filled her with terror. She was a stranger in a strange land. This would normally be the time for a woman to feel joy, but that happiness was meant to be shared with a husband. The father had no desire for her. Damn him. I hate him! But the thought didn't ring true.

Adriana was considering all the appropriate curses she could think of with regard to jackanapes when a knock sounded at the door.

When she opened the portal and saw him standing on the threshold, she thought she might melt into a puddle on the ground and be sucked into the earth. He was here! She took a calming breath and tried valiantly to maintain her reserve. She stepped aside, allowing him room to enter.

"Yes," she inquired, trying desperately to keep the tremor from her voice.

He strode into the cottage, then turned to her. "Adriana. I had to see you."

"Why is that?" Thank heavens she had her pride and was not jumping into his arms and making a fool of herself, though the thought did cross her mind.

"I fear I have done you a terrible wrong. I took advantage of a situation and it was unforgivable."

She stared at him, expectantly. It was as if she might be just anyone and not someone special to him. Would his tone warm to her?

"I am not clear how I can make this situation right. Especially in light of the fact that you so kindly came to my aid." He dropped his gaze, appearing profoundly repentant.

His feelings of regret were not what she desired and Adriana was not impressed with his apology.

"Situation? Do you consider our circumstances a situation?"

"No. That is not what I meant. I am not always adept at expressing myself, but I came to say that I enjoyed our night together on the ship."

"I see." Her heart seized and she fought for control. She repeated the words in her head. *Enjoyed our night together? That was it? Would he now offer to pay for her services?*

"And I am so very sorry I did not see through your disguise. It is to your credit, though, that it was so effective." His attempt at a smile only further annoyed her.

"Why are you here, Captain?" *And why are you not on your hands and knees swearing your undying love and begging for my hand,* she screamed in her head.

"I care what happens to you and—"

"How kind. You may go now."

"You do not understand."

"Oh, I believe I do. You feel some sort of debt or obligation. Well, do not bother. Your apology is accepted I have no need of your gratitude."

"Please, Adriana."

"Please, Captain? Please what—forgive you? I already said I did. Can I help you to absolve yourself more? Shall I demand some sort of payment for our night together and another purse, perhaps, for saving you from Melanie Cabot?" Her voice rose in direct proportion to her rage.

"This is not going the way I envisioned."

"Well, I am so sorry to hear that. Please go before I feel the need to say or do something I will come to regret. And do not bother to return."

Defeated, he took a step back and turned away. At the last instant, he turned back, his expression pleading, but she made sure her expression conveyed implacability. The door closed just before the tears cascaded down her cheeks.

***

Robert's anger at himself knew no bounds. He had come in all sincerity, with naught but love in his heart. It had taken some soul-searching to admit he was besotted with the woman. He'd come determined to say so, but instead of expressing it, he had treated her like a woman of the night. How could he be so inept? If she did not feel the same, perhaps he could convince her, entice her somehow? Might he be bestowed a second chance? What could he do? It was possible she could be more forgiving and amenable with proper wooing. But how could he woo her if she would not see him?

He had known from that first night that she was one of a kind. It was not just that she was beautiful. She was smart and strong and, looking back, she had been so kind to his crew. They adored the old woman.

Why had she come into his cabin that last night? There could be no explanation other than that she was drawn to him. She had responded with incredible passion to his caresses and driven him mad with desire. It was clearly not her wont: she had been a virgin.

Yes, she did love me then. Maybe I can help her remember that emotion. The thought cheered him. *Now I must find a way to stop tripping over my own tongue and let her know I feel the same for her.*

He pulled himself up on the black stallion that paced in impatience, reflecting his master's distress. The animal leaped forward and ate up the miles home. Robert gave him his head, absorbing the soothing rhythm of the run.

By the time he reached home, he had calmed and went directly to seek his mother. She was sitting at the small desk in the dayroom, writing a letter, surrounded by the golden light of late morning. She looked up. "Robert?"

"I am in trouble."

Elizabeth raised her eyebrows.

"I have done something stupid."

Patiently, his mother kept silent.

"It's Adriana. I am in love with her." When Elizabeth didn't react, Robert was surprised. "You know?"

Elizabeth laughed. "I think you are the only one who did not. So, what help do you need?"

"I went to talk to her, but I made a mess of it."

"You have your father's charm. He never did say the right thing. It is a wonder we ever got married. Did you tell her you love her?"

"No."

"Why not?"

"I tried to. Do you think that would have worked?"

"Could you have done worse?"

"No. But, I don't think she will listen to me now. I treated her like—"

"Of course you did. And now you must find a way to make it right. Do you wish to marry her?

Robert thought about this for a moment. "I think I do."

"Then you must tell her. You must propose. Find the moment and seize it. Honesty is the only path now. I love you, but you are not the best at expressing yourself. Stop tripping over your tongue and just come out with it."

"I love you, Mother."

"I know."

Chapter Nineteen

Adriana took great joy in riding Cinnamon. She relished the pleasure of the horse's powerful muscles stretching out and soaring over the thick green grass. Birds must feel this way, unfettered by the pull of the earth. Next to her, running to keep up, Blossom's tail wagged with delight. The pup was growing by leaps and bounds.. Caring for the two animals filled the time and gave Adriana great satisfaction. Even cleaning Cinnamon's stall was not so much a task as it was a loving gesture.

She tried not to think of the disappointment of Robert's visit. When he had appeared, she had been so hopeful but, of course, it had come to naught. She had to face the truth of the matter. Robert Stuart had no interest in her other than a feeling of gratitude. There was to be no future with him. She devoutly wished something could change that fact, but she must accept it. She had crossed an ocean alone and relied on her wits to protect herself from the threat of her stepmother, so she knew she would find a way to manage.

Some mornings, after feeding the mare and Blossom, Adriana ventured to the farmer's market. She touched the firm, ripe tomatoes and sniffed the perfumed aroma of the fat peaches. They made her mouth water. The corn glittered gold in the sunlight, lined up like soldiers showing off their uniforms. Fresh herbs scented the air: mint and oregano, basil, and parsley. Adriana cataloged recipes in her head.

Embroidered towels and carved utensils beckoned, next to fired clay pottery and hand drawn signs of welcome. Adriana would wander among the stalls, touching this, smelling that. She took her time, hoping to catch sight of the captain. But someone like him wouldn't be in a market, would he?

Tate became a frequent visitor to the cottage. His presence eased the loneliness. He spoke of this and that, but skillfully avoided any mention of the captain. She hated to admit that she longed to hear of the man. She was just torturing herself over an unworthy bounder, but still the yearning gnawed at her.

Had she been unfair to Robert Stuart? After all, he had tried to—to what? Ease his conscience? He had bedded an innocent and then required she save him. Of course, he must feel guilty. But guilt was not love, and it was his love she desired.

Signs about the town announced a public summer picnic on the town hall green and Adriana busied herself in the kitchen. If there was one thing that would impress, it was her cooking. She put a pan of beans in water to soak and combined spices and chunks of beef into a savory mixture. She simmered the beans for hours so the flavors would meld. Soon the entire cottage was filled with the most delicious aroma. A wave of nausea came over her and she ran from the cottage to the side of the house to spill her breakfast in the grass. It took a moment to catch her breath. What made me so sick? I don't want to miss the picnic tomorrow.

After a few minutes, the wave passed and she felt

herself again. In fact, she was hungry. Starving. It would not be amiss to sample her own cooking, would it?

Excited the next morning as she walked with her contribution to the center of town, she tried to control her hopes of being accepted. The nausea had threatened again, but she'd controlled it.

A huge table, aching with pans and bowls, cakes, and pies, dominated the center of the park. Proudly, Adriana set her pot next to another. A woman came up behind her and stepped forward, blocking Adriana's view of the table. When she stepped away, Adriana's food had been moved down. Another woman appeared and pushed it still farther down on the table. Finally, a third shoved it to the edge. It fell and splashed beans and beef onto the ground. The three women walked away as if naught was amiss. Adriana's jaw dropped at this affront. How could they be so rude? So cruel? Tears scalded her cheeks as she ran home to her cottage. The humiliation was visceral and she felt sick to her stomach. Why had she come to this terrible place? Why did they hate her so?

One afternoon, Tate and Hazel came to visit and Adriana was delighted.

"I brought her for a cooking lesson. I hoped you would share some of your vast knowledge." Tate raised his eyebrows with hope in his expression.

Hazel glared at him, but smiled at Adriana. "Mr. Tate seems to takes great delight in reminding me, and everyone else, that I have no skill in the kitchen. He seems to think it's just 'cuz I do not try. Do you think so?"

Adriana laughed with delight. "It is certainly possible. Some people just are not comfortable preparing food. I was almost raised doing that, under the tutelage of one with great talent and instincts. We can certainly try to improve your abilities if you wish." She turned to Tate. "Have you still not engaged a proper cook at the house?"

"We make do. But the captain just growls at whatever is placed before him, so no one is of a mind to do more than the basics. He seems to be ever in a foul mood."

Adriana was secretly pleased to hear this. She wondered if she was the reason for his misery. Sad that the man was still constantly on her mind. Had she been unfair to him, or misunderstood his words? Her hopes rose at the thought, but—he had not come back. If he wanted her, would he give up so easily?

Hazel returned frequently. Adriana tried desperately to teach her to cook, but the big woman seemed unable to prepare even the simplest dish. So, they often spent the afternoons with Adriana cooking and Hazel sampling. And they would both end up laughing at Hazel's bungled attempts at the art of cookery.

Tate seemed to know instinctively when food was ready and magically appeared just as the savory stew or hearty soup was ready to be devoured. Adriana had to admit that their appreciation of her talents was having an effect on her own eating habits—lately she had been starving. At night, that is. She reasoned that was because she had been so sick every morning.

One afternoon, Hazel turned to Adriana while she was chopping vegetables. "How are you feeling, Miss Adriana?"

"Fine. Why?"

"You look a little green around the edges."

Adriana was taken aback. "Well, sometimes I am sick in the morning. How did you know? I would worry I have contracted some disease, but I am ravenous come evening and I find myself desiring the oddest foods. Did you know that corn with syrup is delicious?"

"Child, did your mama not explain these things to you?"

"Mama died when I was twelve." Adriana's eyes filled with tears. "Oh, Hazel, you do not think I am truly ill?"

"No, child. I think you gonna have a baby. You do have all the signs. You are sick in the mornings, you eat like a man at night and you have been getting thick around that tiny waist. When was the last time you had your monthlies?"

"Oh, my God." Adriana gasped in horror. She knew she had missed her courses for at least a month, perhaps two, and she was sick in the mornings, but she had hoped it was due to the changes in her life. To hear it spoken out loud gave it reality. She was carrying a child. His child. But it could not be. They had made love but once. He did not care about her. That was obvious. What was she to do?

"That is ridiculous," she said, hoping to convince Hazel. "Surely it takes more than once to conceive a child," she said, clinging to denial.

"If it is meant to be it only takes the one time."

Hazel opened her arms wide. Adriana fell into them and sobbed until she was exhausted.

Afterward, Hazel sent her to wash her face. When she returned, Hazel said, "It will be fine, I promise."

"What does that mean? How can this possibly be fine?"

"It means I know who is responsible for your condition and I intend to see right done by you."

"You will do no such thing! I would not have him

come to me now. If he wanted me, he would have made it clear long before this."

"The man is just stubborn. I know he cares for you. He always asks after you. It is just his head is too swelled to come here. But I know he cares."

"How can you be so sure?"

"I have my ways. I have known that boy since he was a newborn."

"Well, even if you are right, he will have to decide I am the one he wants and come to me himself, on his own, without obligation. That is the only way. So, please, promise you will not tell him. I want your word. Please." Tears threatened to spill down her cheeks again.

"If this is what you want, I promise. But child, he has a right to know."

"Right? What right does he have?" Adriana fairly screamed, then abruptly closed her mouth. The truth reared its ugly head. "This is all my fault. I disguised myself and then got angry because I was successful. I was the one who went to his cabin. I am responsible. I turned him away when he came to see me. I was cold and unfeeling. But he doesn't care. He didn't come back. He didn't try again." Anger rose and shoved away regret.

"Do you love him?"

Adriana was suddenly filled with an emotion that felt much like anger. "Love him? That arrogant, pompous, unthinking, uncaring—"

"So you do."

"What difference does it make? He clearly does not feel the same."

"I do not know that to be the truth. I think you are both so pigheaded. I just want to see you cared for and happy. A man should be made to see to his responsibility.

But, if you do not want me to tell him, I will not. Not my place, anyway. But I sure hope you come to your senses and tell him yourself. Just because he is prideful does not mean you should be."

"It is not pride."

"Whatever you say. Now, if you ever need anything, just send one of the local boys to fetch me." A quick hug and Hazel was gone.

Adriana sank back into the sofa cushions, bombarded with emotions. She felt alone and confused and frightened, but there was a certain pleasure and joy in knowing a human being was growing inside of her. It had certainly been conceived in love—at least on her part, and she suddenly felt very warm.

Chapter Twenty

The sunlight filtered in through the cottage window and painted the room in muted golds. Adriana laughed out loud at her dog. Blossom was valiantly attempting to jump on the bed with her. Adriana picked up the pup and hugged her.

"Okay, little one. Although you are not so little anymore. I will put you out for your morning walk and then we shall have breakfast. I actually think I can eat this morning."

Adriana strode to the front door. She opened it a crack to let the dog slip through. "You go ahead. I need my robe and slippers. I dare not been seen with just my thin nightclothes." Blossom stopped at the threshold and looked back to her mistress.

"Okay, just give me a moment to dress." Adriana ran back into the bedroom and threw on an old gown.

They walked together in the warm morning air, happy to be alive. Adriana found a stick and tossed it for the dog who gleefully ran after it and brought it back. The game continued for a while until Adriana's stomach reminded her it was past time for breakfast. She was hungry now all the time, no matter the time of day.

"Time to go in, Blossom. Come on, girl." But the dog had disappeared behind a bush on the side of the house. "Well, you shall be back soon enough when you realize it is time to eat."

Adriana headed into the cottage and made a plate for the dog, then brewed tea and sliced some bread. She left the door open but when Blossom didn't appear, Adriana peered outside.

Blossom stood on the top of a nearby hill. A large shadow near her appeared to be a man on a huge, black stallion. Was it her imagination? The thing sat motionless among a stand of tall trees. Squinting, a man did come into focus. His dark cloak was pooled behind him and he had the look of a sleek, black hawk perched on his horse. Blossom, however, was not intimidated. She rubbed her muzzle against his outstretched hand until he pushed her gently back toward the house.

Adriana called to the dog, unnerved. She could not identify the man and it sent a shiver down her spine. Who was he and what business did he have with her dog? Blossom ran to Adriana who grabbed her, hugged her hard, pushed the pup into the cottage and ran inside. Shutting the door, she fixed the lock. She would have to be more careful letting the dog outside.

Later in the afternoon, there was a knock on her door. Adriana was not really surprised as Hazel had promised to come by often, but the woman on the threshold was not who she expected. Elizabeth Stuart stood there smiling and Adriana swallowed her shock. Elizabeth was a handsome woman. Her eyes were the same bright blue as those of her son, but Adriana was convinced that, unlike her offspring, her gaze missed nothing. The woman exuded a kind of determination, but there seemed to be no arrogance to her. Adriana thought Robert must have inherited that trait from his father.

111

"Come in, come in." Adriana stood back so the woman could enter. "I did not expect you. May I offer you some tea?" Adriana was impressed by the older woman's bearing, but the lack of warmth she exuded gave Adriana pause. What had changed? Where was the grateful woman from a few weeks ago?

"That would be lovely." Elizabeth swept into the cottage. She scanned the room, then turned back to her hostess. Elizabeth was dressed in a fashionable day dress of striped, green satin, her matching flower-laden hat perched at a jaunty angle on her head. She had dressed carefully for this visit.

"Please, be comfortable." Adriana gestured to the sofa.

Elizabeth sat with her hands folded in her lap while Adriana prepared the refreshments and returned bearing a tray. Then, she looked at the older woman expectantly.

"Well, I suppose I should simply come to the point. I have been waiting for you to return to our home and yet you have not come." Her direct gaze was as no nonsense as her statement.

"I do not understand." Adriana was genuinely confused. "Have I forgotten an appointment?"

"You appeared that night to save my son from the manipulations of that Cabot girl. And then you disappeared. Robert has buried himself in work ever since and seems forever in a foul mood. And I had to wonder as to your price."

"Price… for?"

"Rescuing him."

Adriana bristled at this accusation. "How dare you. I appeared that night because I could not sit by and watch a terrible injustice. Doing the right thing should not be met with insults."

112

"Forgive me." Elizabeth leaned forward, her eyes shining. "But I had to ask."

"I suppose you do not know me or my character, so it is understandable, I suppose."

Elizabeth lifted her gaze and sat back, her posture more relaxed. "So what is going on?"

"I don't get your meaning."

"I have been told my son failed to recognize you once you lost your masquerade. Which must have been a terrible rejection and left you with little but anger and resentment."

Adriana could not help but smile at this woman's candor. "Yes," she responded, the simple word clearly conveying so much.

"But there are pieces missing. I am old, but neither stupid nor blind. When you came to our house for dinner, I could see how my son looked at you. And how you looked at him. I can only judge by his temper that he wants something he cannot have. I should apologize for spoiling him as a child, but it is much too late for rectifying things." Elizabeth smiled at the attempted humor in this remark. "I understand he offered you employment as our cook."

"Mrs. Stuart—"

"Elizabeth—"

"Elizabeth, I had no need of his pity."

"I assure you, it was not pity. He appreciated your talents and I'm certain you know by now our table is lacking. But I assumed that was taken as an insult, although I am clear that was not his intent. We are desperate for someone with the ability you displayed and he only knew you as the old cook."

"Because he is—forgive me—blind."

Elizabeth nodded. "His father was the same. A wonderful man, but simple."

"I do not know what you seek from me."

Elizabeth looked directly at Adriana's waist, now a bit wider and rounder and lacking the confines of a proper corset. "To be honest, I am not sure. I waited for you to demand compensation for your appearance that night, but you did not. And I can see from your home that you are comfortable. Hazel has spoken of you with such genuine warmth that I believe you have good character. But the mystery is driving me mad."

"Mystery?"

"Why are you not with my son? Is it possible you carry his child? Do you really believe this city will welcome a single woman with child? Clearly you are of good breeding, so you cannot fool yourself into believing your life will be anything but isolated and reviled. And, although he might have hurt your feelings, certainly enough time has passed that you should forgive him."

Adriana pulled herself up straight. She was not sure if she should be resentful or merely just be direct. It was clear that Elizabeth did not know for certain that Adriana was enceinte and she was fishing for confirmation. Hazel had kept the secret and Adriana was pleased. "I am not sure what you are suggesting. As far as anyone is concerned, I am a widow. My husband died on the crossing."

"As for your widowhood, I have heard that story. And I have no faith it will make you more acceptable. My dear, you have done me and my son a great service, and I do not wish to see you ostracized. I have come to offer my help. Especially now that I can see your motives are without blemish."

"You are very kind, Elizabeth, but my problems are of my own making and I shall solve them."

114

"So you do not deny you are carrying *my* grandchild. Do not bother fabricating the non-existent dead husband. According to my son, you were a virgin and I doubt you have had the opportunity for any kind of tryst since your arrival."

Adriana felt herself blushing, but kept silent.

"There is more?" Elizabeth prodded. "I can only surmise you have reason for the deception you created."

Without warning, Adriana's emotions bubbled up beyond containment. Tears coursed down her cheeks and the story poured forth. "Elizabeth, your son does not care for me or he would have attempted to make things right."

"My dear, it is clear to me that my son is madly in love with you, but he is too headstrong to admit it. I am sure he fears rejection and, like all men, cannot easily manage a blow to his ego such as that. He had a bad experience when he was younger and more impressionable, and it appears to have left deep scars. I had hoped he'd recovered sufficiently to accept real love when it appeared, but I truly believe that accounts for his hesitation. I do know he tried to make things right with you, but obviously was unsuccessful."

"He merely sought to soothe his guilt."

"No. I do not believe that. I do not profess to know the details of what passed between you at his visit here, but I do know he was bereft. He sneaks out and rides here to check on you at every opportunity."

"How do you know that?"

"I am his mother. I have my methods."

"I still feel he is motivated by guilt and I do not want him because he feels he owes me something."

"And you cannot be so foolish as to think your life will be anything but hell if you bear a bastard."

"No one will know. I will continue as a widow. I

have not used my maiden name. And, I have sufficient means to support myself and a child. I did not take this journey unprepared."

"Yes, but when you embarked on your journey, was having a child a consideration? There is so much more to it than you can possibly imagine. Trust me. I have learned from experience. It is not all cuddles and kisses."

"No, of course not. But I will love the babe and care for him and he will want for nothing. I will see to that."

"By the way, what is your real name?"

"Booth. Adriana Booth. I took the last name of a childhood friend to ensure my anonymity on the voyage. But I beg you, Elizabeth, not to intervene. I am fearful of the consequences of my actions, but I worry more about having your son tied to a woman he has only chosen because of circumstance. And now, hearing some of his history, I am even more determined to stay my course."

"You do love my son. Well, I give my word. I shall not tell him of your condition or pressure him, but it will not be a secret for much longer." Elizabeth looked pointedly at Adriana's waistline, which made Adriana's cheeks burn. "And then, you will have to confess. This is a small community and there are no such secrets held for long. When that time comes, you will have to peer into your heart and test the strength of his love. And trust me, you will know. Then, only you can decide where your future lies. Adriana, I believe you to be an honorable and strong woman. I give you my support, no matter your choice. But do not be so stubborn that you shoot yourself in the foot, if you take my meaning."

Adriana laughed. "It seems that subtlety is not your best quality."

"That is true. But lack of it has always saved me so much time."

Chapter Twenty-One

Adriana was home. She was surrounded by her parents and they were all laughing at some elusive joke. They were all so happy.

Then, the darkness fell.

When she opened her eyes, her face was wet with tears. Blossom trotted to her and put her paws on the bed. The dog's warm tongue licked away the dampness. Then, she nuzzled against Adriana's neck.

She stroked the dog's soft, tawny fur and smiled sadly as the memories faded. Suddenly, there was a scream of pain from outside. She grabbed her bed robe and ran to the door.

A riderless horse was tearing down the road. As it disappeared around the corner, something moaned in the bushes. She turned and nearly fell over a lump curled in a small mound of earth to the right. A young boy looked up, his face contorted with pain. He was eight or nine years, at most, but was bravely holding back the tears that threatened to spill down his freckled cheeks. It was the same child she had seen passing by her cottage on many an afternoon. Her heart went out to him.

Adriana leaned down and helped him sit up. He groaned and grasped his left thigh. The lower leg was resting in a very unnatural position. There was no doubt it was broken.

"My name is Adriana," she said. "And I would appreciate it greatly if you could escort me back into my cottage, for I am most uncomfortable out here. You see I am not properly attired. And you strike me as a gentleman. Perhaps, if I aided you in standing on your uninjured leg, you could help me."

The boy smiled through his pain. "I will gladly aid you, Madam. Just give me a moment."

Bravely, he stood with Adriana's help and leaned on her as they half-walked, half- hobbled inside. Blossom followed behind. Adriana guided him to the sofa and settled him back on the cushions and the dog plopped next to him on the floor, alert.

Adriana hurried to draw the blankets from her bed and covered him, although the room was warm. She feared the shock of his accident might drain the heat from his body. In her cupboard, she located a bottle of brandy, poured a healthy draught into a glass, and carried it to the boy.

"Drink this. It will help with the pain. What is your name?"

"Brian. Brian Woodley."

"Well, Master Brian, you are very brave. A weaker man would not have been able to withstand pain such as this. And only a gentleman would have been kind enough to save me from the embarrassment of being seen improperly clothed. So, I thank you for that. Now drink."

Brian smiled weakly. He took a swallow and coughed and choked as the fiery liquid made its way down his throat. She withheld her grin, then indicated he drink some more. "Just take it slowly." After several more swallows, some of the pain and tension left his face. Then, she eased him back into the pillows.

She walked to the hearth and searched the woodpile

for two fairly straight pieces of wood. Then, she pulled a petticoat from the armoire and proceeded to shred it into strips. When she returned, the boy's eyes were a bit glazed and she prayed he had drunk enough brandy.

"Master Brian, I need to stabilize your leg. Then, I shall find a doctor. Do you understand?"

The boy nodded.

Gently, she eased off his boot. His body stiffened with the movement, but he made no protest. She grabbed scissors from her sewing box and cut away his pant leg, exposing the injured member. The break had not penetrated the skin, but it needed to be straightened.

"Brian, I am going to have to move your leg. It will hurt greatly, but if I do not, you may never be able to walk right, as it will not heal properly."

Brian closed his eyes and clamped his jaw shut. Adriana took hold of his ankle and pulled. His scream of pain unnerved her and tears coursed down her cheeks, but the worst was past. Blossom jumped up, her ears standing up straight at the sound, but she settled back down when Brian relaxed.

Adriana braced the leg between her knees and laid strips of cloth alongside his skin. Then, she placed the pieces of wood on either side of the leg, securing them by wrapping more strips of cloth around them. The leg now immobilized, she raised it slightly and supported it with several pillows.

Treatment complete, she tucked the blankets tighter about the boy. Soon, his face softened with sleep. She donned a cotton gown and pulled her chair up beside him. Blossom lay at her feet and together they stood watch over their patient.

It was later in the afternoon when Blossom nudged

her arm, urging her to wakefulness. She stretched stiffly, the long hours in the chair taking their toll. She rose and went about some chores. She was making tea when he groaned. He tried valiantly to sit up and grinned through a gap-toothed smile when she entered the room.

"Good afternoon, Master Brian. How are you?"

"Better, thanks to you. It still hurts a bit, but I think you are a pretty fair doctor. How did you learn to fix legs?"

Adriana smiled warmly. "My father was a doctor. He taught me some things he thought I might find useful someday. And, sure enough, you were kind enough to break your leg so I could practice on you."

"I would say it was my pleasure, but my parents told me never to lie."

"Well, I certainly understand. I shall get you some tea and biscuits and then go and tell them where you are. I can only imagine they must be terribly worried."

Brian nodded. "My mother will probably be in a fit." He hesitated a moment and swallowed as if the next words were having difficulty finding voice. "I wish to apologize to you."

"Apologize? Why?"

"I have been rude. So many times I rode by and you greeted me and I did not respond in kind. It was impolite and I am sorry."

"I accept your apology. I suppose newcomers are not easily welcomed here."

"Especially when they are young and very pretty." Brian blushed bright red at this.

"So, where is your house?"

"It is the big, white one… if you have paper, I can draw you a map."

"That would be very helpful."

She returned with pad and a quill and ink, then brought a tray with tea and scones and honey and he ate hungrily, relating details of his accident as he shoved food into his mouth.

It seemed he had been riding by when a shadow jumped from the bushes near her cottage and his horse reared. He explained he had been caught off guard, since normally he had an excellent seat and would not have fallen.

The thought of someone lurking about her house sent a shiver up Adriana's spine. She walked outside and was unnerved to see a set of large footprints in the loose earth near the window. A flat place under the window spoke of someone kneeling there. She squatted and realized she could see directly into the house. The memory of a gunshot coming through her window flashed bright. She quelled the panic that rose. Who would be interested in watching me? Sarah Jane could not possibly know where I am. Adriana hugged herself for reassurance and strode back inside.

"Blossom is wonderful company," she announced. The pup thumped her tail. "She will watch over you until I return."

Armed with Brian's map, Adriana saddled Cinnamon and they rode off.

***

The Woodley estate was situated just north of the city. It sat squarely in the center of several acres of very rich farmland. Tobacco plants stretched as far as the eye could see and their leaves glowed a deep green in the rays of the late afternoon sun as they swayed with the gentle breeze.

121

The approach to the house was sheltered with massive oak trees that arched in a canopy of light-filtered branches. She might have compared the residence to her home in England, but she realized that those thoughts would only make her homesick.

She dismounted at the front of the house. A young man seemed to appear out of nowhere and took Cinnamon's reins. "I shall not be long, so you need not take her to the stables." The boy nodded and stood holding the mare while Adriana went to the front portal and lifted the heavy brass knocker.

The door swung wide and a dour-faced black butler glared down at her. "Yes?" he demanded, none too politely.

"Are the Woodley's at home? I have come about their son, Brian."

"Brian?" a voice shrieked from inside. A woman ran to the door and nearly pushed the butler aside. "Where is he? What have you done with him?"

Adriana smiled at the well dressed, handsome woman whose face was contorted with suspicion and worry. "Done with him? I have given him aid." Adriana kept the anger from her tone, as she understood the woman must be crazed with concern over her son. "He is at my cottage. I came as soon as I could leave him. He fell from his horse and broke his leg."

The woman reddened immediately and lowered her head. "I am so sorry, Miss…"

"Mrs. Hadley. Adriana Hadley."

"Mrs. Hadley. Please, come in. I was just so worried." The woman's eyes filled with tears. "When his horse returned without him…" Her voice was choked off by a sob. "Is he safe? I shall send for the doctor immediately."

"His leg is set and he is indeed safe. The break does

122

not appear too serious. It should heal nicely. I splinted it, but I am sure you will still wish a doctor to see it."

"Can I go to him?"

"Of course."

"My husband is searching for him now. I must send word he has been found. I am so sorry for my rude behavior. Please forgive me. I owe you a great deal. I am Ruth, by the way." Ruth gave Adriana a quick, unexpected hug, then hurried to don her cloak and call for her carriage. Cinnamon was secured behind and Adriana gave the driver directions.

As they drove, the women exchanged pleasantries. "It is lovely here this time of year," Adriana said.

"How long have you been in Virginia?"

"Since the beginning of summer. I am a widow. I lost my husband on the voyage from England. It was far more difficult than I imagined it would be."

"You have my condolences. And, yes, the romance of an ocean voyage and the thrilling sense of adventure does fly out the window when faced with storms and cramped quarters and the unknown. It must have been so difficult. Why have I not met you?"

"This is not the most welcoming of places," Adriana tried valiantly to keep the bitterness from her voice.

"Well, we shall have to change that. There are gatherings planned I shall see you are included in all the celebrations."

Chapter Twenty-Two

After much hugging and kissing and tears, which embarrassed Brian greatly, the women helped him to the carriage. Ruth swore her eternal gratitude to Adriana. She watched the carriage until it was no longer visible and went back inside. Suddenly, her home had grown very quiet.

Adriana was left with the unnerving thought of someone peeping at her and she placed the gun on the table within easy reach. The feel of the heavy metal lent some reassurance. She closed the drapes tightly and made certain the door was bolted.

She slept fitfully, visions of dark shadows looming from all directions. She woke with beads of sweat on her forehead and lay back on the pillows, breathing hard. *Today, I shall go shopping. I will not confine myself behind a locked door. Enough of being frightened. I hate that part of me.*

As she rode down the main street in the morning, she sensed a different atmosphere. People smiled at her, waved, greeted her with a 'good morning'. She reined in the horse at George Peyton's office and as she entered, he jumped up and greeted her more expansively than usual. Taking both her hands, he asked as to her welfare.

"I am well, thank you, Mr. Peyton."

"All these visits. You certainly must call me George. How can I be of service this fine morning? More jewels to sell?" He had been solicitous, but this day he was so much more. "I must say, you are looking radiant."

"What has happened?"

"Happened?"

"I have come into town so many times in the past and been either completely ignored or received glares. This morning, however, people are going out of their way to wish me well."

He cleared his throat. "Your act of kindness to one of our most prominent families has earned you a high measure of good will. It is not easy to gain acceptance when one is new and unknown."

It took a moment for Adriana to register this information. "You mean young Brian? I did no more than help a child in need. It was not particularly heroic."

"Well, everyone else seems to think it was. You did well to treat him with such care."

"Well, if I had but known it would take so little to win over the populace, I would have found a child and rescued him sooner."

Peyton frowned at this, the sarcasm lost on him. "I do not think I understand."

"It was a jest. But as to the reason for my visit today. I have need of more funds." This time she handed over a bracelet of diamonds and rubies.

"You seem to have an endless supply of resources. I say that not suspiciously, but because I am impressed."

"My late husband was very generous. Also, he believed that jewels would be easier to transport then cash. He assumed it would be a simple matter to convert them if it became necessary. And they are so easy to wear."

125

"He was a wise man. You must miss him terribly."

"Yes, yes I do." But the one she actually missed was but a few miles down the road.

She took her leave of Peyton and made her way to the dress shop. The dressmaker ran forward to greet her. "Miss Hadley, so good to see you. What can I do for you this morning?"

An hour later, the dry goods merchant's reception was similar. "Miss Hadley, may I deliver your purchases today? It would be my pleasure."

A woman she recognized from the picnic stepped up to her and Adriana clenched, ready for some insult. "Oh, Mrs. Hadley, I haven't had the time to apologize for the mishap the other day. I have no idea how your dish fell from the picnic table, but I am sure it was a terrible loss to us all. Perhaps at our next event, you can recreate it." The woman smiled with apparent sincerity. "I am Flora Swanson. And I hope you can come for tea one afternoon."

No idea how the dish fell? Come to tea? Laughing to herself, Adriana thought she must remember to buy gifts for Brian and his parents.

The remainder of her day was spent going from shop to shop. She passed a merchant featuring clothes for newborns in delicate patterns. Pinks and blues and yellows beckoned. She should buy some gifts for her babe. She would name him Adam. As to the last name—her thoughts were drawn to the baby's father. Ocean blue eyes and his hands—strong and capable and—so gentle. And how she missed him and desperately wanted to—what? Have the man beg for forgiveness? Would she forgive him? Yes. Without a second thought. But, obviously, he does not wish to see me. Well, damn him, then. Damn him for not loving me. It was an oft repeated refrain in her head.

Adriana realized her eyes had filled with tears that threatened to spill down her cheeks. She blinked quickly to force them back and swallowed hard. She smiled as if she had not a care in the world, for how would she explain suddenly bursting into tears? Then again, her 'husband' had just died at sea. As her heart was dying now.

Chapter Twenty-Three

A knock sounded on the door of the cottage. Blossom lifted her head, then settled back to her nap.

"Some fine watchdog, you are."

The dog wagged her tail in response and Adriana rolled her eyes.

She flung the door open and was surprised to see a boy of about thirteen. "Well, good morning. And who might you be?"

"Johnny, ma'am. I have here a note for you. I was told to wait for your reply."

"Well, come in. Can I get you some tea? A cookie, perhaps?"

The boy's eyes lit up at the prospect of something sweet and Adriana went to fetch him the snack. While he nibbled, she opened the envelope. It was an invitation from the Woodleys for a party two weeks hence. It was to be a formal affair and they would be honored to have her in attendance.

Adriana was delighted. She took pen to paper and graciously accepted. This she handed to Johnny, then bid him wait a moment. She handed him some coins and wrapped a large chunk of chocolate cake in a piece of linen. He seemed pleased by both the money and the treat and hurried on his way.

She closed the door and leaned back against it. A party! She needed something to wear. She could cook, but she had never been able to sew and needed to get to the dressmaker for something special. *Yes, I must remember to do something else very nice for the Woodleys.*

***

Adriana was nearly shaking with excitement and anticipation. The dressmaker had delivered a glorious gown of gold brocade, cut low enough in front to highlight her décolletage without being too revealing. Her breasts had gained more fullness and she worried about looking too daring. She had had the dress cut full, as she had no intention of wearing a corset tight, and it cannily concealed her expanded middle. She swept her hair into intricate curls, weaving gold ribbons among the blonde locks. A simple necklace of gold, and matching earrings and she was ready. The question kept desperately pushing its way into her thoughts: would he be there tonight? It would be a crashing disappointment if he did not appear. *How can you continue to pine for this man? You had a one-time encounter. You are destined for disappointment.* But then, how could she—or anyone—erase such a memory when his child lived within her?

Adriana had hired a carriage for the evening. The driver gave a quick intake of breath as she stepped out of the cottage and he helped her inside the coach.

Strolling into the foyer of the Woodley's beautiful home, she was immediately face-to-face with the blue eyes and handsome features that had occupied so many of her thoughts and dreams. Was it an accident that he was at the door when she arrived, or did she dare think he had been waiting for her? His eyes swept over her almost possessively and with obvious pleasure. Her heart began to pound and her breathing grew fast and shallow. For a moment, she felt faint and prayed he did not notice, although she was sure her cheeks flushed. He was here! Damn him!

He reached out to cup her elbow. Instinctively, she stiffened, and tried to pull away. But he held her firmly.

"I pray, do not make a scene," he whispered in her ear. "But I must speak to you in private."

A thousand responses went through her head, but all she could do was let him lead her to the library, just to the left of the foyer. The room was dim, illuminated by a scant few candles that highlighted the bookshelves and massive wooden desk. He closed the door and turned to face her. "There are no words I can say. I have wracked my brain—"

"Your small brain."

"Granted. My small brain. But when you appeared that night and told me you could never forgive me and to never touch you again… And then, when I came to speak to you and could not manage to find the words I wanted to say… Adriana, you have plagued my thoughts."

"Plagued? Interesting choice of words."

"Please, do not make this more difficult than it is."

"Difficult—for you? I was the one abandoned. You did not have the good grace to recognize me after that last night on the ship. I have had to conceive a lie to explain my situation and of course, condition and—"

"Condition?"

"Do not tell me no one has told you." Her tone was full of disgust. "You have not even tried to make things right. Not that I was interested in any offer you might make. I hate you!" Her pulse throbbed in her temples and blood raced through her veins.

He stepped up to her, his eyes piercing hers and his lips a mere breath away. His voice was a husky whisper. "No. You do not hate me. I can see it in your eyes. You are in love with me."

"Why you arrogant, fatheaded, pompous—" His mouth cut off her curses. The kiss was filled with passion and longing. Her lips opened and his tongue plundered her mouth, teasing, arousing. His hands moved everywhere and settled on her waist. When he felt the soft roundness, he pulled back, his expression one of awe. "You carry my child?"

"Do not act the fool. Is that not why you have accosted me?"

"No. I, as you so delicately put it, 'accosted you' because I am in love with you. And I have been since that night on the ship. You have tormented my thoughts, my dreams. I cannot concentrate for the memory of your skin, the touch of your hair, the scent of your perfume. I tried to take you at your word that night when you came to my home and spoke for me, but my heart could not let you go. I did try to talk to you after that night. Do you not remember my humbling myself at your door? But I failed to properly express myself. Since I am clearly not effective with prose, it was suggested I use actions and not words to woo you. I was hoping that tonight there would be safety in numbers and you would, at least, give me the opportunity to declare myself by doing what I have meant to do since the beginning."

"You did not know of the babe?" Her eyes narrowed in disbelief

"How would I know?"

"There are some who might have mentioned it."

"Who? Who would dare keep such a secret from me?" His eyes widened in anger.

"Those who kept my secret did so because they knew I did not want your pity or your charity."

"You are so hard-headed. Did you not hear me before? I love you, woman. How many times must I say it? I love you! I have never cared about another woman like this and it has driven me completely off balance." Then, his voice softened to pleading. "Can you just show me some kindness in return? Some pity? Please? Especially now that we will share this child? Which, by the by, makes me incredibly happy."

She saw the honesty and the fear of rejection in his eyes, but trepidation held her back. "If it is true, what you say, then what took you so long?"

"Ask my mother. She will agree with you that I am an ass."

"I like your mother."

"And she likes you. But we digress. Answer the question."

"Question?"

"Will you marry me?"

Adriana's breath caught in her throat and she thought for a moment she might faint. "M-m-m…"

"Marry me," he re-stated, as if talking to a dull-witted child. "I have planned this night for weeks and prayed you would show me some sympathy." He dropped to one knee and took her hand in his. "So, will you—marry me?"

"You do not even acknowledge me for weeks and tonight you propose?" Even as she said the words every fiber in her being wanted to rush into his arms. She desperately wanted to believe him, to trust.

"Just hear me out. I actually believe I fell in love

with the cook, Mary. It was so strange, but when I first saw you, I felt drawn to you. I wracked my brain—"

"Your so small brain—"

He ignored the jibe this time. "As I was saying, I tried desperately to assimilate what I was feeling, since you were an old woman."

"Not exactly the kind of woman who generally attracts your attention?"

"That night, when you appeared in my cabin, there was something so familiar about you and yet, so exotic. It was not until you appeared at my home that I began to understand my own heart. And by then, I knew I had been a fool."

"I cannot disagree."

He stood, but didn't release her hand. "I have often wondered what caused you to come to my cabin that last night. Was it perhaps you wished to be with me? I am hoping that was the reason."

"More likely I mistook my way in the dark." She tried to sound caustic, but it was difficult when he seemed so sincere and vulnerable.

"I know I deserve your sarcasm and worse, but Mary—Adriana—I am bereft without you. Please. I beg you. Marry me."

The words penetrated the wall she had so carefully built. Tears filled her eyes and ran down her cheeks. Was this possible? Did the man who had occupied her thoughts and dreams really feel the same? She had spent so many hours desperately trying to push him out of her mind, out of her emotions. Knowing it had been her pain that hardened her heart. she held her breath, closed her eyes and took a leap of faith. There were no sufficient words, so all she could do was nod.

From his pocket, Robert withdrew a small box. A diamond ring surrounded by sapphires glinted in the candlelight. He slipped it on her shaking left hand. Then, he kissed her, so fervently, so passionately, he had to support her weight as her knees forgot to hold her upright. All the suppressed emotion and desire was channeled into her response to him. It was miraculous the room did not catch fire with the heat between them.

After a time, she gathered her wits and pulled back, trying to catch her breath. She sighed deeply and closed her eyes. When she opened them again, he was smiling with all the love he truly felt. "You have made me the happiest man in the known world."

"I do love you, Robert. I have loved you since I first laid eyes upon you." Pressing her lips together, the blush of embarrassment heated her cheeks. "I used to squeeze into a small space on deck so I could watch you work."

"I yearn to hear that tale. I want to hear everything. But tonight I wish to show you off, since you are more than beautiful. You are magnificent, an angel come to earth and I am blessed among men."

She smiled and she knew her face was alight with happiness. "So, what now?"

"Now, my love, we join the party and celebrate."

Walking on clouds, she followed his lead into the main room, which had been cleared of furniture. It was a lovely room, with pale blue damask on the walls and a table pressed against the wall, heavy with food. Candlelight shone on the beautiful dresses and the jewels and the heavenly scent of fresh flowers filled the air. Sweet music played. Had there ever been a more glorious setting?

Robert held his hand at her waist. Adriana was

introduced to so many she hoped she could remember at least some of their names. But they all seemed to know her and many congratulated her on her care of young Brian.

"Yes, everyone in town is aware of your heroics," an older man said.

"Please. It was truly so little."

"You do not understand. It is no secret the people here can be… rude… to newcomers. And a beautiful and unattached young woman will certainly not draw favor from the wives. Which means you cannot draw support from the husbands, either. Notwithstanding, you helped one of their children. You stepped in and took the higher ground and these people are decent enough to recognize it."

As if summoned, Ruth Woodley appeared from the crowd. "Adriana, I am so happy you accepted our invitation." She was gowned in a pale purple satin dress that sparkled with crystals.

"Thank you for asking me. How is Brian?"

"Well on the road to recovery. Cranky that he cannot ride or enjoy other activities for a few more weeks, but there will be no aftereffects, thanks to you. As a matter of fact, the doctor was amazed at your prowess. How did you ever learn to set a leg like that?"

"My father was a doctor."

"Yes, now I remember Brian mentioning that. You learned well. And you know you have our eternal gratitude. If there is—"

"Ruth, you have already thanked me sufficiently. In fact, everyone in town seems to know my name now."

"We can be a cold, unwelcoming lot and I apologize for that. We colonists sometimes forget our manners. I hope you do not hold a grudge, since I for one, would certainly appreciate the opportunity to be your friend."

"I would like that."

Ruth turned her attention to Robert. "I see you are acquainted with Mrs. Hadley."

"More than merely that. She is my fiancée."

Ruth's look of disbelief was quickly masked with her smile. "I had no idea. Well, my dear," she addressed Adriana, "he is a lucky man and you are blessed, as well." She seemed confused. "But I thought you were newly widowed."

Caught in her lie, Robert came to the rescue. "Her late husband was a dear friend and I had promised him I would always take care of Adriana. It was as if he sensed his own demise, poor man."

Ruth nodded, accepting the explanation. "The Stuarts are a fine family. I cannot wait to have tea and hear all your future plans. When are the nuptials to take place?"

Adriana attempted to respond, but Robert cut her off. "The wedding will take place as soon as possible. We will let you know as soon as the date is set."

After a while, Adriana grew tired. So much had happened and it seemed so unbelievable. She tried to stifle a yawn, but Robert noticed.

"Time to get you home and in bed." He winked.

"Why, Captain Stuart, you think to compromise my reputation?"

He looked pointedly at her waist. "I think it is a bit late to worry over such trifling matters, do you not? Besides, we need some time to ourselves. There is much to discuss and plans to be made. Now that I have you, I never intend to let you go."

After saying the proper goodnights to their hosts, Robert excused himself to dismiss her carriage and summon his own. Adriana stood in the foyer, blissfully unaware of anything but the incredible happiness filling her.

"I warned you, bitch, this is not over." Adriana immediately recognized the whining voice of Melanie Cabot, now filled with venom,.

Adriana inhaled, refusing to allow the other woman to dampen her happiness. But she intended to stand her ground.

"Melanie, whatever you hoped for or believed, Robert has no interest in you. You tried to trap him with lies. That's where you failed. Take your defeat like a lady, if that is possible, and move on with your life."

"Lies? You have conjured one lie on top of another. The house of cards you built will soon come tumbling down."

"Melanie, I tried to be sympathetic, but now you are no more than a minor annoyance. Go away."

Fury narrowing her eyes, the other woman stormed off just as Robert appeared and whisked Adriana out the door.

"What troubles you, love?" he asked, when they were seated in the carriage.

"Melanie Cabot. I don't think she has given up on you."

Robert laughed out loud. "Then that is to her shame. I cannot believe she ever thought I would mistake you for her. I suppose I pity her. She is jealous and not worthy of your attention. Besides, there is so much more to occupy our thoughts this night."

Before Adriana could respond, his mouth was on hers, hungrily demanding. She responded with the weeks of her own pent up passion. His hands caressed her face, then moved to her throat. His lips followed. She, still unschooled in the ways of lovemaking, was unsure where to put her hands, so she followed his lead.

As his hand reached inside the neckline of her dress and cupped a creamy white breast, she gasped. Her entire body trembled with his touch. Taking his cue, she opened his shirt and stroked the skin that stretched over hard muscle.

The sound of a throat clearing had them both jumping to attention. The driver stood with the carriage door open.

Embarrassed, Adriana straightened her clothing. Robert merely shrugged and descended the vehicle, then turned back and swept her into his arms.

"May I come in?" he asked, a crooked smile on his handsome face.

"Why, Captain, I think you must, as the carriage ride has affected your balance. Perhaps you should come in and rest a moment."

Bending his head to her ear, he spoke so only she could hear. "I want you, Adriana, more than I have ever wanted anything in my life."

She laughed. "Your mother said you are spoiled and, therefore, always seem to get your heart's desire."

"You are my heart's desire."

Dismissing the carriage, Robert carried her inside the cottage and to the bed, laying her on the fluffy coverlet. A bark from Blossom made him laugh out loud. "I will not harm her." The pup seemed to accept that and laid down on the floor.

Wherever his hands touched her silken skin, his lips followed. She felt more than loved. She felt worshipped.

He placed small, loving nips on her shoulders. Her gown slipped down and he took one of the hard, pink peaks of her breast into his mouth, licking and sucking. She couldn't keep from crying out. She reached for him, but he brushed her hands away, seeking more exploration.

"You are so much more fantastic and beautiful than I even remembered," he breathed between kisses. "I will never get enough of you."

Adriana was too caught up in the throes of desire to speak. She held on to him as tightly as she could, marveling in the intimate responses of her body. The place between her thighs felt like it might explode. It ached for him to fill the empty void. She arched her hips, pushing into his, begging for release.

Almost reverently, he stroked the small roundness of her belly, then moved down to the juncture between her thighs. He slipped his tongue into the hot, wet space and teased the hard knot of her womanhood. She cried out in surprise as her orgasm almost immediately filled her world with light and exploding stars. She drifted down, muscles letting go, savoring the feeling.

Now it was her turn to give him pleasure. She eased herself over and pushed him into the soft bed. Then, wantonly, she mimicked his actions. She kissed and nipped and licked his body, beginning at his throat and moving down to his waist. A dark line of soft hair pointed the way to his hard, throbbing erection. As her tongue touched his swollen member, he groaned and reached for her. He maneuvered her up so she straddled him. He slipped inside her and she felt every inch of him as softness welcomed strength. He plunged deep and held. Adriana groaned and pushed her hips higher.

Slowly, she moved with him, her body rocking in the

ancient rhythm of love. He guided her hips and she moved faster. Incandescence built higher until it was a fever. An exquisite explosion erupted. She called his name for the world to hear as her welcoming flesh tightened in one spasm after another. Then, he drove himself deeply inside her once more, and his own erupting heat filled her as it poured out.

Slick with sweat and satiated, they lay in the flickering light, holding on for dear life. Blossom stood and sniffed at them, obviously checking their welfare after all that screaming. The pup licked Robert's hand and went back into the main room to lie by the hearth. Adriana looked at him suspiciously.

"Does she know you?"

"Who?

"Blossom. My dog. She acts as though you are an old friend."

The corners of his mouth lifted in a smile. "We have met."

"What does that mean?"

"It means I have—come by on occasion to see that you were safe and doing well."

"When?"

He sighed loudly. "Truth be told, I come several times a week to look in on you."

She digested this information, deciding if it made her happy or angry. If he was here so often, why had not made himself known to her? Before she could ask the question, he answered it. "I was certain you would not welcome my visits, but I had to ascertain you were safe."

"You know you frightened Brian Woodley, hiding as you were in the bushes. You must know his leg was broken when he fell from his horse."

She felt his spine stiffen. "I do not hide in shrubbery. Why would you suggest such a thing? I admit I rode by or perhaps watched from the hills above your cottage. I merely did not wish to incur your wrath."

Adriana thought a moment. "Well, if it was not you concealed, who was it?"

"I don't know. But I shall find out." His tone let her know he was more than concerned by this information. He turned toward her, but instead of speaking more, he moved his lips to hers and began a new exploration of her mouth.

They made love slowly this time, savoring each touch and kiss until the passion built beyond their control and the heat consumed them. Then, there was only light and stars and the universe centered on the place where their bodies came together.

Chapter Twenty-Four

Robert and Adriana were busily planning their wedding. Elizabeth agreed to maintain the pretense of Adriana's widowhood to stop the wagging tongues. And it made Robert seem all the more noble for stepping up to keep his word to care for her.

One day Adriana inquired what he desired for a wedding gift. He had leered at her and replied the only thing he wanted, all the time, was the only thing he wanted, all the time. Did men never think of anything but making love?

Hazel and Tate were delighted the couple had sorted out their problems and were now happy and Robert's mother could not have been more thrilled at the prospect of gaining both a new daughter and a grandchild.

On this particular morning, Adriana woke up slowly, luxuriating in the softness of the bed and the sounds of Robert moving about in the other room. She still insisted he try to keep his visits discreet, although Robert said it was fooling no one. The gossips, however, had plenty of fodder speculating as to the paternity of the unborn child. Most believed the story she had concocted that she had been widowed on the voyage and neither Adriana nor Robert felt the need to correct that assumption.

Robert strode into the bedroom carrying a tray. He

placed a kiss on her forehead. "Hungry? Because I have been to the bakeshop and procured some delicacies for your breakfast." He lowered the tray so she could peruse the choices.

"What a lovely gesture. Thank you, sir. I am, indeed, starving. I have been freed from the sickness in the mornings and now seem to be hungry all the time. However, there is enough here for an army. Will you still love me when I am fat and lumbering about?"

"I will love you until the end of time." He placed his hands over his heart to insure she knew it was a vow.

"I will hold you to that."

He smiled at her and sat beside her as she delicately chose a cream-filled cake. She beckoned him to lie down. Then, she squeezed the cream on his bare chest and proceeded to lick it off. "I believe in sharing."

It was much later in the morning when his thoughts were clear. "I do have a question, love, since you never told me how it came to be that you were on my ship in the first place. Dressed as you were—are you a fugitive?"

"If that were the case, would it matter?"

"No. I would have to escape with you from the long arm of the law or go to jail alongside you. But I doubt that is the case."

"I am a fugitive in a way. Not from the law. From my stepmother."

"I do not understand."

Adriana poured out her story. She stopped only to sample bites of the delicious food and sips of tea. When she had finished, she took a breath. "I had no choice. My life was at stake."

"That is indefensible. But you need never worry again. I will see to it you are never threatened by anyone or anything, ever."

"How can you do that?"

"I have contacts in England. I shall send word that this matter is to be resolved. There is no reason for you to have had to flee for your life. Your stepmother will be punished for the harm she has caused."

"It is not important that she be punished. I just want to rid myself of the threat."

"Money corrupts. It makes sane people do insane acts. That is no excuse and she must be held accountable for her greed. Not to mention the wound that was inflicted."

"I suppose you're right."

"It shall be known that Adriana Hadley—soon to be Stuart—is protected and safe and no one dares molest her."

"Booth."

He looked at her quizzically. "Booth. My surname is Booth. I only used the name Hadley to hide my identity. Jason Hadley was a childhood friend, so I took the liberty of using his name as my own."

"Then, I must go to my solicitor and see matters taken care of. Would you care to accompany me into town? Or perhaps you fear being alone in a coach with me?" "

She smiled seductively. "My lord, do you think of nothing but your most base desires?"

"If you were not a vixen who has robbed me of all rational thought, it would not happen."

"Then, we shall ride horses to town and you will not be tempted to indulge in lusty actions."

"Just talking is enough to seize my imagination and make me want you. If we are to leave this small haven, I suggest you discuss the weather or some equally innocuous subject immediately."

"Warm today, is it not? I expect we shall see rain before nightfall." They laughed aloud together.

***

They spent the morning apart, Robert with his lawyer and Adriana at the dressmaker. She could not believe that her life was so filled with dreams coming true. The noon hour came and Adriana met Robert at the hotel on Main Street. Lunch was ordered and she ate like one starved. She gobbled up meat, vegetables, and bread. Her eyes lit up as a tray of sinfully rich desserts was wheeled past their table.

"I am amazed at your appetite. Where does all the food go?

"It goes, my lord, to nourish your son. Blame him, as it is definitely his doing."

"You are convinced it is to be a son?"

"Aren't you?" She fixed her gaze on the tarts and cakes on the table nearby.

"Are you tired?" he inquired solicitously as they left the hotel. "I do not wish you to overdo."

"Oh, did you wish me to save my strength for some other activity?"

"You are an evil baggage to think of nothing but making love."

"I am not the one who thinks such thoughts constantly. And you are so arrogant your ego will prevent you from entering buildings, as your head is so large. Can you behave?"

"No. I do not believe so. If I did, you might tire of me. Admit it."

"I admit nothing," she said.

Leslie Hachtel

"Well, my love, although it pains me greatly, I must tend to my business affairs. I shall escort you home and perhaps you can take a nap or—perhaps have a small bite to eat as you must be ravenous. Then, I shall return to escort you to my home for supper after concluding my work. I cannot allow you to become emaciated."

She slapped him on the arm, laughing. "It is a good thing I love you."

He shook his head. "I do fear it is tarts you love these days. I shall be grateful when my son appears and you can preoccupy your thoughts with things other than food."

"You are my nourishment. I love you, Robert," she said, her voice husky. She wondered if anyone had ever been as happy as she was at this moment.

Chapter Twenty-Five

Robert strode through the front door and greeted Jamison, standing stiff and formal as ever at the door. The English butler had been with the Stuarts for years and his old world manners bespoke of a time when formality was the order of the day.

"Good afternoon, Jamison. I would like a bath before supper. And we shall have a guest for the evening meal."

"Yes, sir. Good afternoon, sir. You have visitors in the library."

He looked at Jamison quizzically. "I am not expecting anyone. All right, please send in some refreshments." Robert was annoyed at this distraction as he had intended to occupy himself with more business matters before he needed to call for Adriana.

Melanie Cabot sat primly on the sofa next to a young man. Her face broke into a malevolent grin as Robert entered and her escort stood to be introduced. Robert was singularly unimpressed. The man stood nearly a full head shorter than Robert, with mousy brown hair pulled back from his pasty white face. His brown eyes, however, suggested a cunning intelligence. He seemed to have an air about him that bespoke more years than his appearance conveyed and there was a cruelty in the set of his lips that made Robert immediately wonder as to his character.

Melanie's nasal voice cut through Robert's assessment. "Captain, may I present Jason Hadley. Jason, Captain Robert Stuart."

Before Robert could respond, the maid appeared with a tray bearing coffee, tea, and cups, which she deposited on a small table. She curtsied and disappeared. The distraction gave Robert a few moments to think, but he could not fathom the purpose of this visit. He found Melanie completely distasteful and could only wonder what she was plotting.

Robert did recognize the accompanying man's name. He suspected it was not a coincidence. This must be the childhood friend to whom Adriana had referred. But why was he here? Nothing was making sense. His thoughts jumping from one possibility to another, he took a seat in a chair across from the two, waiting for an explanation as to this visit.

Melanie's voice cut into his reverie. "Captain," she said, her voice dripping with poisoned honey." It is so good to see you again. Please allow me to properly introduce my companion. This is Adriana's husband, Jason Hadley. I thought, since you and I are old friends, it might be more pleasant if I was the one to accompany him here."

Robert had suspected something, but these words hit him with unexpected force. He glared at Melanie. "What nonsense is this?"

She merely smiled with satisfaction. Her knife had clearly hit its mark. "Nonsense, Captain? I think not. Since his name is Hadley and so is hers—that woman."

"That woman's name is Booth. She only borrowed his name…"

"*Was* Booth. And you believe her deception? It would make sense that she never bothered to mention a husband. Jason has told me everything." Reaching over in mock sympathy, she patted his hand. "Poor man. To be so betrayed by a heartless woman."

Robert turned to the younger man, an eyebrow raised. "And you agree that this is the truth?"

Jason grinned, his victory clearly sweet. "It is."

"I see. I suppose you have proof of your claim?" Robert's voice was tightly controlled, now, as he faced Jason. The younger man squirmed under Robert's perusal so he looked to Melanie for encouragement and when she nodded, Robert did not miss the exchange.

"And you suddenly appear to make your claim? Why now?" Robert asked, controlling an urge to violence. Jason swallowed hard, his Adam's apple visibly bobbing in his throat.

"Adriana is my wife. We were married some months ago and afterward we—had a disagreement. She fled and obviously gained passage on your ship. When I realized what had happened, I booked a voyage and am here to reclaim her." Jason's voice shook slightly, but he did not stammer. "My marriage vows are sacred to me and I cannot turn my back on them. I love her and she is mine."

"I see. So, when did you arrive in Virginia?"

"Last week."

"You were so anxious to, as you say—reclaim your wife—but for an entire week you have not yet made her aware of your presence? How is it you happened upon Melanie? It strikes me as very odd."

"I was lucky enough to meet her soon after I disembarked. She was most obliging. It was a lucky coincidence that she was acquainted with both you and

149

Adriana. She thought if she interceded, it might make my path easier."

"Why should she aid you?"

"Because I felt sorry for him," Melanie jumped in. "Abandoned as he was and all alone in a strange country. I took pity on his plight. Because that's the kind of person I am." Straightening her spine, she lifted her head in self-righteous pride. "I could not in all good conscience allow him to see that dreadful Adriana without offering some caution."

Bristling at her words, Robert sought to control his response. "I see. It strikes me as one hell of a coincidence. I fear you have lost credibility. I thank you for the afternoon's entertainment, but I have business to attend to. Jamison can show you out." At the mention of the butler's name, he appeared at the library door as Robert stood and turned to leave the room.

"Well, it really matters not whether you believe him or not. The facts remain. They are married and that is that," Melanie called to his back.

Robert turned and glared at her malevolently. "I am unsure of his game, but *your* motives are obvious," he spat at her.

"It is not our motives you should question."

"Truly. Enlighten me, Miss Cabot."

"She wants your money, of course. Is there ever enough money for a woman like that? Poor Jason here was not wealthy enough to suit her and she hoped to better herself. Perhaps you seemed an easy mark. After all, men become such fools when a woman is willing. If you know what I mean."

"She has a scar," Jason piped up. "On her left shoulder. A gunshot. How did she tell you she came to have it?"

Robert just stared at him, clearly unnerving him, but Jason continued. "Well, the truth is she was shot in a hunting accident some time ago, but I can only imagine she added some drama to her recollection. Adriana is beautiful and charming, but she has always had trouble distinguishing the truth. Perhaps she told you the tale of her wicked stepmother bent on assassination. Of course, that is only one in her repertoire."

Robert was unconvinced. Adriana had said she had known Jason since childhood, but the scar on her shoulder did not appear to have been there for very long. The skin was still pink and had a raw look. He could only wonder what was actually going on here. What was Jason trying to gain? Although Melanie's motives were obvious. She had been humiliated and women such as she would never forgive such a slight.

Keeping his own counsel, he continued waiting to hear something with enough truth to make him question his beloved. Melanie was an annoyance, a troublemaker. It had to be a fabrication.

"Robert, there is the detail you continue to overlook. She uses the name Hadley. Why Jason's name?"

He narrowed his eyes at Melanie and a muscle in his jaw jumped with tension. He turned to Jason whose gaze had dropped to his muddy boots, then turned away in disgust. "You are not welcome in my home. I trust you will not darken my door again. Or that of my soon-to-be-wife. Am I clear?"

Melanie smiled nastily. "Oh, you are clear as glass. But, before you dismiss us out of hand, you might want to look at these." Melanie victoriously moved to him, the silk of her skirts rustling in the quiet room. She held out a sheaf of papers and shook them nearly under his nose.

Robert snatched the documents, none too gently, and read them, not bothering to cover his irritation. His eyes widened with disbelief as the words on the pages registered. He had no reason to doubt the authenticity of these English documents of marriage. Before his eyes, on the rough parchment, was evidence that his beloved Adriana was indeed wed to the sorry excuse for the man who stood before him.

His chest ached as though a knife had been thrust through his heart, but he concealed the agony. He would not give them the satisfaction of knowing they could claim victory. Adriana had lied to him, betrayed him. Perhaps the child was not even his. The child. Suddenly, it made no sense. Adriana was a virgin that night aboard the ship. Her blood on the linens was the quiet proof of that. So, even if the documents were authentic, the marriage to this man had never been consummated. Which meant it was not valid. The man had a weak claim at best. It was as simple as filing an annulment. He needed to meet with his solicitor first thing in the morning and he would see this matter to its conclusion.

Still, he needed answers from Adriana. What had caused such desperation that she felt she needed to wed this sorry excuse for a man? And did he pose such a threat that she needed to disguise herself and flee?

"Now are you convinced?" Melanie asked, sweetly.

"I am solely convinced you are a viper and this little man has somehow agreed to throw in with you. Perhaps he has reasons of his own. This has raised more questions than it has satisfied. As I said before, you are not welcome in my home. Jamison will show you out." With that, Robert strode from the room and up the stairs to the privacy of his chamber.

Chapter Twenty-Six

The bath water was less than soothing, but Robert sat in it until the water cooled, unlike his temper. He had been running the events of the past hour over in his mind and had to admit there was some veracity to the man's story. He had seen the documents with his own eyes. Of course, Melanie would join him in his quest. The woman was full of hate and underhanded plots. But what was Jason's motive? Did he wish to claim Adriana, no matter how unwilling she was? Why would Jason want a woman who so obviously did not desire him? The documents appeared real. Was Adriana really his wife? Did she wish an annulment? She must. Robert had no doubt she carried *his* child, conceived on the ship. Perhaps she invented the fear of her stepmother because she was ashamed of the truth. Why would Adriana have married the man in the first place? Why would she still have been a virgin unless she meant to invalidate the marriage?

He did not trust Melanie or the pale faced little man. But what if Adriana had actually been married to him, as the documents made clear? That would mean she had played him for a fool. Disguised herself to gain passage on his ship. Let him fall in love with her. All to escape that mealy mouthed husband.

An impulsive or gullible man would believe the tale

that had been presented to him. However, with a closer inspection, it made little sense. Adriana lived well and clearly had resources of her own. Was it possible she had taken money from Jason. No, Melanie said Jason was not wealthy. So many questions and so few answers he could trust.

The true question that plagued him—was this history repeating itself? Another Rebecca. Another manipulating female who had used him and was probably, even now, sharing her amusement with others. It was unimaginable that he could again be so naïve.

Is there not a decent female in the world? Are they all out for their own ends? Do they never consider the man's feelings? The other women in his life always seemed to have an ulterior motive: marriage to a wealthy man. It mattered not if they loved him or cared for his welfare. They merely wanted the rich life he could provide.

But those others were not Adriana. She was different. He knew in his heart she truly did love him for himself. So, there must be an explanation.

The frustration gnawed at him. He drove his fist into the water and gained no satisfaction when the water sprayed out onto the floor and walls. What was truly going on?

He rose from the tub and wrapped a warm linen towel about his hips. He took another towel to dry his hair, all the while formulating plans. He was not a man to avoid a confrontation if one was necessary. He must go to Adriana and ask for the truth. It was the only fair thing to do. She needed the opportunity to explain and he had to admit, he wanted an acceptable reason for the visitors this afternoon.

He trusted Adriana—or at least had trusted her. Could he be so wrong?

The warm late afternoon air washed over his face as he cantered to his destination. He tried over and over to pin down his thoughts and form them into a cohesive pattern, but it eluded him. He knew he needed to separate his emotions from the soon-to-be discovered truths or he could be caught in a maelstrom from which he could never escape. He tried to list the facts as they had apparently unfolded. But his heart kept interfering and reminding him of his love for her.

Adriana opened the cottage door at his single, hard knock. "You are early." One look at his face caused her to take a step back. "What is it? What troubles you?"

"Are you married?"

She looked at him as if he had just grown another head. "Married? Not as yet." Suspicion narrowed her eyes. "Robert, what are you asking?"

"I had visitors this afternoon. Your dearest friend, Jason, accompanied by none other than Melanie Cabot."

She just looked at him, completely baffled. Finally, she responded. "Jason? Jason Hadley is here—in Virginia? I am confused. Why? And with Melanie Cabot? Why would he seek to visit you?"

"To demand his rights, of course."

"His rights—to what?" She appeared completely confused.

"To you. He says he's your husband."

She laughed out loud. "My husband! You jest." Seeing his expression, she immediately sobered and stepped back further from the door. Motioning him inside, she sat down on the sofa while he took the chair across from her. "Please, tell me what has transpired."

"You do go by his name."

"I told you why. It was to protect my identity."

"I saw the documents."

"The documents?"

"Marriage documents."

"What? That is ridiculous."

"So you are saying they were forged?" He so wanted to believe her.

Adriana laughed. "Well, they are certainly not real. They must be forgeries. I don't know why he would claim such a thing. He was supposed to be my friend."

"How would he come by counterfeit papers?"

"Ah. That has been an art form in England since before patents of nobility were required. Coins to the unscrupulous can provide nearly anything. But that still leaves the question—why."

"To convince me to leave you? Does he want you for himself?" Not that he would blame the other man.

"He did propose before I left home, but I had no interest and I told him so. This is a lost cause for him. Thank God you came to me and didn't believe him."

Looking deep into her eyes, he knew she was telling him the truth. Relief poured though him like a balm, and he nodded. "I will seek him out and find his motive. And there is no question as to Melanie's. I give you my word, you are safe from them both."

He stood and angled to the door. "I will be back in an hour to pick you up for dinner. I have some inquiries to make." Anger surged through him and he needed to find Jason and confront him.

"Be careful."

Robert smiled. "My love, you have no need to under-estimate me. I will uncover their plot and see an end to it."

She stepped up and kissed him on the mouth as he pulled her close. "I will return in an hour," he repeated.

***

Adriana sat at her dressing table getting ready for dinner. The hour had dragged, but Robert would be here soon to pick her up. Worry about his confrontation with Jason preyed on her, but she had faith Robert would prevail.

She knew Jason wanted her for his wife, but to go to such extremes to follow her across the ocean and concoct a such an outrageous fantasy? What could he hope to gain?

Maybe Jason believed she would be at odds here, all alone, with no champion, and willing to return to the sanctuary of her home. Adriana smiled. Clearly the man didn't know her as well as he believed.

Putting Jason and the hateful Melanie out of her mind, she gazed into the mirror imagining the future, then closed her eyes. She and her captain would sail the world. With their children. Lost in reverie, she jumped when Blossom uttered a low growl. Looking up, she saw a shadowy figure reflected in the mirror, standing behind her. A man. At first, she thought it was Robert and smiled. Immediately, she realized her mistake. She cried out and abruptly turned.

It was Jason behind her.

He remained in place, just staring at her. Blossom continued to utter guttural sounds, threatening.

"Send the mutt outside."

The hair on the back of Adriana's neck tightened. Fear congealed in her center. Suddenly she knew, without doubt, Jason was dangerous. Jason? She took a deep breath, summoning bravado. "Well, you have saved me the trouble of seeking you out on the morrow. I have some questions and I require answers."

"Are you not happy to see me, my love?"

Leslie Hachtel

"I am not your love. I have no idea as to your game. What do you want? And how did you get in my house?" Jason being here explained the strange footprints outside her window. There was now no doubt who had been crouching outside her front window. Jason had been spying on her. The thought sent shivers up her spine.

"You are, as ever, too trusting. The door was unlatched. Now, send the dog outside so we may talk. Or I will shoot it where it stands." He withdrew a pistol from his belt and it flashed silver in the candlelight. Adriana choked.

Terrified, she took hold of Blossom's collar and pushed her out the door. Then, she faced her intruder.

He smiled, poison oozing from him. "You cannot escape me, after all."

"Escape you? I don't understand. It was not you I ran from. And how did you find me?"

Jason smiled malevolently. "Did you think yourself so clever I could not? A man can always find the information he requires. And a few coins spread about on the docks had a man telling me about an old woman slipping aboard a ship bound for the colonies. I, however, am not so naïve that I believe everything I see. I knew it had to be you."

"But why, Jason. Why follow me? What do you want? I have told you I have no wish to marry you. And why would you tell Robert we were wed? What could you gain?"

Jason laughed cruelly. "Why, you, my dear. Who do you think shot you? How else could I convince you that you were in danger and needed my protection? But then you ran off, which I did not foresee. Annoying."

It took a moment for the information to permeate her

addled brain cells. "You shot me? It was you—not Sarah Jane? Why?"

"I did not try to kill you or you would be dead. You forget my expertise with a pistol. I was merely attempting to convince you." To emphasize his claim, he stroked the barrel of the weapon.

"Of what?"

"That Sarah Jane was a threat." He shook his head in mock sorrow. "Poor Sarah Jane. Cold as the grave. I could not take the chance she would refute my tale, now could I?"

The horror of his words was unfathomable. "You shot me? Killed Sarah Jane?"

"It was her own doing. She came to me and wove a sad tale of how her wretched stepdaughter had robbed her of all she was entitled to. She asked my advice." He shrugged. "I assured her she would have no more worries."

"She sought you out to offer her aid?"

"I was formulating a plan to convince you you needed me when she sought me out and explained she had been living in an old cottage on my property. Terrible conditions for a lady to tolerate, but she had nowhere to go. She was so desperate for someone to help her. She thought she had found in me a willing ally and I did not disabuse her of that notion. We agreed to meet the next night to make arrangements for her to reclaim her rights."

"You both conspired against me?"

"I suppose you could see it that way. She was not a terribly clever woman, just one filled with greed."

"You took her life? How could you?"

He shrugged. "It was not as if it was my first time. There were others. Do not forget to add my first wife to the list."

Adriana's mouth dropped open. "Your first wife?" It took her a moment to reconcile this revelation. "So that's where you were those years you disappeared. But why? Why would you do such terrible things?"

"Money, of course. The bitch didn't leave enough of a legacy to sustain me. I have very expensive tastes. I found myself again in the position where I needed to rebuild my fortune. And you were so wealthy it boggled the mind. I thought all I had to do was frighten you into marrying me. You were such a gullible child. There was a time when you looked up to me and would do anything I suggested. I counted on that. It was meant to be a simple thing."

"But I did not cooperate."

"No, you did not. Yet. But there is still time."

Now it was Adriana's turn to laugh. "How do you plan to accomplish your goal? I will not marry you."

"Again, not as yet. You see, at this moment I am already burdened by a new wife. But that should not take long to resolve. It is a big ocean between here and home."

Adriana was both shocked and confused. "A new wife? That you plan to kill?

"I believe you are acquainted with the lady. And there is no love lost between you. Melanie Cabot. I mean, Melanie Hadley. It was a lovely ceremony. Her father was so proud—and relieved. He even readily agreed to finance our honeymoon."

"How did you manage to find her?"

"I made sufficient inquiries. It astounds me how much people love to gossip. Why the tale of Melanie Cabot and her rejection by the Captain in your favor set so many tongues wagging. Then it was but a simple matter to seek her out and offer my sympathy."

"Jason, you cannot mean what you say. You are right, I do not hold any affection for her, but she does not deserve the fate you have in mind."

"That is not for you to decide."

"You can lay claim to her fortune as her husband. I know she is rich."

"True. But why would I wish to be cursed with the woman if I can avoid that lot? If she is gone, I am free to call her fortune my own once her father is dead and then claim yours as well. Besides, she is so unappealing, the thought of the marriage bed forces my gorge to rise."

Adriana could not believe her ears. Was he truly confessing to being so greedy that nothing and no one would act as a deterrent? Could any one man be so cold and unfeeling? "How much money could you possibly need?"

He laughed and the sound was harsh. "Why, all of it."

"And how is this to play out for me?

"For now, you are going to run away—again."

"What?"

"Yes, my love. We are going home. Once we land on the sweet shores of England, you shall marry me in actuality."

"Why would I do that?"

"There are two reasons I can name. Shall I?" he taunted her.

"Do."

"First, I have sufficient funds to have hired an assassin that even now watches your captain. If, after we arrive back in England, I have not sent word that all is well, your beloved Robert will be killed."

"Oh, God, no." Adriana felt sick. Robert killed? It was unthinkable.

"Fear not. He will live if you do as I say. I have nothing personal against the man. Only that he could yet be an impediment to my plan. Once you and I are truly wed, he poses no threat. Until then, I must have options to rid myself of him."

Jason was obviously enjoying her torment. "Second, I could kill the child you carry before it is born. You are pregnant, aren't you? It remains no secret. You see, I plan to be with you as your devoted spouse, until the time comes. Then, the brat will be under my control to do with as I choose. I thought of ridding myself of the child sooner, but I fear you might succumb if I do. So I shall wait. It will give me the time to use you myself if the spirit so moves me. And it might actually amuse me to have a child." He shrugged. "We shall see as to its fate after it appears."

The words made her gorge rise. Maybe he could be reasoned with if she could keep him talking. "Why are you telling me all this now? Do you hope to scare me?"

"Yes." He hesitated and grinned, the sight sending terror through to her bones. "Have I succeeded?"

Fear down to her core suffused her. This man, whom she thought her friend, had just threatened everything dear to her in life. She must acquiesce—what choice did she have?

"What would you have me do?" She locked her hands together to stop their shaking and hoped to reason with him. She must think clearly and wait for an opportunity to escape this madman.

"Pack. Gather your things. We sail tonight. You will not cry out or attract attention. You must know what I'm capable of. Do you understand?"

Adriana nodded. When Robert came to get her, he would see she had flown. He would question why she would leave. Certainly, he would take care of Blossom and Cinnamon. She prayed Robert would not think the worst of her.

Adriana packed some clothes and essentials into a bag, making sure she scattered various garments on the floor. Jason took hold of her arm and roughly escorted her out of the cottage.

Blossom was crouching near the door outside and issued a warning bark. Jason kicked at her and Adriana screamed. The dog darted behind some bushes as Jason pushed Adriana into the waiting carriage and climbed in behind her, then signaled the driver to move. Adriana hoped the man might later report what he had seen, but she feared he had been well paid for his silence.

Adriana thought she would be sick. She stared out the coach window, unseeing as the miles sped by. How could this have happened? Why? Everything had been so perfect.

Adriana had seen a madness in Jason's eyes, an unreasoning. What had happened to her good friend? What would become of her and the baby? Knowing she must do as Jason ordered to protect Robert, she prayed for escape so she could at least warn him of the threat.

The air grew pungent with the scent of the sea and Adriana knew the carriage had approached the dock. Jason intended to force her aboard a ship.

Robert? The ache for him permeated her being.

Would she ever see him again? Maybe Jason's threats of hiring someone to kill Robert were empty? Unsure, she intended to comply, at least until she could find a way out of this. The air was warm and humid, but she was shivering with fear. The man next to her was deranged. She stared at his profile in the moonlight. The same features, but it was if a demon had possessed someone she had known most of her life. The play of light shifted and his face distorted. Terror rattled her very being.

A few crew members populated the deck, intent on their work, but no one greeted them as he led Adriana onto the ship, to a stairwell and down to the lower deck. He pushed her along the corridor and opened a door at the end. Adriana noticed the luxurious accommodations as she was shoved into the cabin. A wide bed covered in a soft comforter might have looked inviting under other circumstances. A table with two chairs squatted in the corner, laden with a basket of fruit and sweetmeats.

A woman had her back to the door and was railing at a young boy who looked intimidated, his gaze focused on the floor. "Unpack my trunks and hang them in the armoire. Be careful, you stupid brat. And get me some tea. Be quick. I am a countess and I expect better service than—" Melanie stopped in mid-sentence as Adriana was shoved into the room and Melanie turned to face her. "What the hell is she doing here?" she demanded of Jason.

"My love, you remember Adriana. I told you I had some business to attend to."

"What business? I am your wife. What do you need her for?" she sneered.

"Countess?" Adriana raised her eyebrows.

"You stupid girl. My husband is titled. I am both married and a countess. What can you claim? A bastard child?" Melanie sneered and turned back to Jason. "Why is she here?" she repeated.

The sounds of the ropes and the clatter of the anchor chain vibrated the room. They had cast off.

"Because I brought her here. That is enough."

"Who do you think you are to speak to me in such a manner?"

"Your husband. And you will not question me again. Are we clear?"

Melanie snapped her mouth shut.

"He plans to kill you." Jason and Melanie both whipped around to face Adriana.

"Don't be ridiculous," Jason countered. "You are just jealous since I chose Melanie over you."

"Melanie, I know you have no reason to trust me, but he means you harm. He just wants your money."

"You bitch! You are beneath contempt. You would take everything from me. You are a mean-spirited witch and nothing more. Jason loves me. Don't you, my darling?"

"Only you, my love."

"Where is *she* going to sleep?" Melanie demanded.

"On the floor at the foot of the bed. I need her and cannot risk letting her out of my sight."

The women watched Jason withdraw a length of chain from a bag on the floor. He clamped one end around Adriana's ankle and the other around the base of the bed, which was fastened to the floor.

"Jason, this is our marriage bed."

"Yes, my dear. How much sweeter to have a witness to our love."

"I don't think I can—"

"Suit yourself." Shrugging, Jason strode from the room. Melanie followed on his heels, slamming the door. Adriana was alone. She could not swallow and her body was deflated. Sweat ran between her breasts, although her hands and feet were ice cold. All she could do now was pray.

Chapter Twenty-Seven

Approaching Adriana's cottage, something struck Robert as odd. Feelings of dread increased his pulse and he was immediately alert. A sound and a movement caught his attention. A whimper and Blossom approached him, her head nearly scraping the ground, her tail tucked tightly between her legs.

Quickly dismounting, he reached his hand out to the pup who threw herself against him. "Where is your mistress?"

Blossom whimpered ever louder.

Robert withdrew a pistol from his saddle and quietly approached the cottage. Candlelight flickered in the gloom and he called out her name, but there was no response. The floor of the bedroom was strewn with articles of clothing, which was very unlike the usually neat Adriana.

Realizing the cottage was empty, he raced out to check her horse. Cinnamon looked at him expectantly, her food trough and water empty. Gathering some hay, and fetching some water for her, his original feelings of trepidation increased a hundredfold.

In his heart, he knew no matter what Adriana would not abandon the creatures she doted on. Someone had coerced her and, checking to make sure the pup was tucked safely inside with proper nourishment, he jumped on his horse and headed to the Cabot's lodging, determined to get answers.

***

"We sail as soon as possible," Robert told Tate, his voice shaking with rage and impatience. "Gather a crew and see the Windstar ready immediately."

"Captain?"

"Adriana has been taken. Jason kidnapped her. I went to collect her for dinner and she was gone. Clothes were strewn all about. Her pup was outside, crying, and her horse had neither fresh hay nor water. She would never neglect them."

"Who is this Jason?"

"Apparently a friend from childhood that only wishes to betray her and cause her harm." Fury tightened his core.

"No one witnessed the departure from her cottage?"

"No. No one saw her. I went to Cabot, thinking Melanie may know something. He informed me his daughter was sailing to England with her new husband, Jason Hadley."

Tate was confused. "Jason Hadley, Adriana's friend, and Melanie are married? But then why would he go after Adriana?"

"I don't know. But I am sure he has her. She's the one he wants. It makes sense."

"No, Captain, it makes no sense."

"Trust me on this. I just know. Adriana has disappeared. She would not go on her own or leave her animals. This is the only way he can control her, since he knew he must get her away from me. And when I find him, I intend to kill him for this. Now, don't just stand there. Prepare to sail."

***

The voyage was so interminably long and boring. The time had flown when Adriana sailed on the Windstar, but she was constantly occupied. Of course, there was the distraction of Robert. For a tiny moment she allowed herself to remember how her heart pumped hot blood through her veins whenever she caught sight of him. He looked and smelled like leather and sea, air, and man. She remembered how he made love to her, touching her most secret places and arousing a passion in her she had never even imagined existed.

This time, she slept on the floor each night and listened to Jason snore and Melanie complain. In the morning, Jason would shove a privy bucket at her and the two would leave, presumably for breakfast. Jason would return with food if one could call it that. Dried beef and hardtack biscuits constituted much of the fare. Melanie spent all day away from the cabin and returned only at night. She would kick at Adriana and laugh, then coo to Jason and beg him to touch her, but the man ignored her. One night, Jason returned alone.

"Your wife is detained?"

Jason stared at her. "You are deranged, woman. I have no wife. And none will say different. The magic of enough coin."

Adriana's head pounded and there was a rushing in her ears. "Melanie is—?" She could not summon the words.

"Who is Melanie?"

Trying to kiss her on the lips, Adriana turned her head away from Jason in disgust.

"No matter. You will still obey me. And after a time, you will welcome my attentions."

Standing arrogantly in front of her, he took off his clothes and laughed when Adriana closed her eyes rather than view his naked body. Slipping into bed, the room immediately resounded with his snores as Adriana collapsed into sobs. She cried for Melanie, but she had to admit she wept more for herself. There was no longer any doubt that Jason was without mercy. If he could throw his wife into the depths of the sea, he had no heart. And if a man had not a shred of humanity, what was there to stand as an obstacle to him?

Sometimes, Adriana's thoughts touched on the threat of an assassin awaiting Jason's word. Unsuspected, one man could easily slip past scrutiny and lay in wait for his instructions. Adriana had little experience with killers. Now she realized that men would go to any lengths for the right price. The thought of Robert hurt, or worse, tortured her. That, combined with worry over her baby, made sleep elusive most nights. Other times, she would assure herself that Robert was a strong and clever man who would not simply go down as the victim of another. That thought brought comfort and some manner of peace.

On this trip, the storms tormented as well, and Adriana prayed for relief. The hideous rocking and screeching of the masts was terrifying. Then, there was truly no rest, except in fits and starts, and food refused to reside in her stomach. She would cling to the leg of the bed and tighten every muscle to keep from screaming.

In the midst of her terror, she squeezed her eyes shut

and pretended Robert was there, feeling their child grow and move, holding her safe from the onslaught, muttering sweet and reassuring words. Adriana imagined how their wedding might have been. That thought brought hot tears to her eyes and the drops made sad trails as they coursed down her cheeks.

Finally, nature's fury abated and the seas calmed. But Adriana still called upon her dreams and memories of her love to see her through the days.

Chapter Twenty-Eight

Windstar had made excellent time across the Atlantic, despite the storms and rough seas. Robert had been relentless, pushing her as hard as possible. Once landed, he and Tate had made inquiries. They had been directed to Bereston, so they immediately gained horses and rode north.

Bereston Manor had been a gift to Adriana's family from Charles I. The king had taken a tumble from his horse one day, bruising a rib. Adriana's grandfather, David Menlow Booth saw to the tending of the King and had earned the King's undying gratitude. Charles, whose belief in the Divine Right of Kings, declared that he answered to no man, arranged for David to become Sir David and granted him an earldom with all rights and privileges. That included the manor, whose previous occupant had recently, and conveniently, vacated the property. Or perhaps fled. No one dared ask.

When the manor loomed ahead, both Robert and Tate gasped. "I knew she had wealth, but I had no idea."

"Maybe you want her for *her* money?"

Robert narrowed his eyes at the man.

They kicked their horses up the drive. The residence was dignified in its age, with ivy winding up the stone walls, as if showing its affection for the structure that supported it. The massive doors were flanked by oriels, the panes of bright glass lending a rainbow of colors to the dusty ground, coaxing it to vivid life.

Robert was the first to dismount. The main structure stretched in a straight line, forming a crossbar for the east and west wings. To the left, and slightly below it, the stables rested in a meadow, the massive size and cleanliness of that area suggested the family's love of fine horseflesh. Robert remembered the beauty of the mare Adriana had purchased in Virginia.

He turned back and glared up at Tate, who was still sitting comfortably astride his mount. "Well, are you coming?" Robert demanded.

"Oh, aye, Captain. By all means." He smiled as he slid to the ground.

A groom ran forward and took their horses as they approached the entrance to the house. The doors were swung wide by a butler who reminded Robert of Jamison. "My name is Captain Robert Stuart and this is my first mate, Tate. We are newly arrived back on English shores and we have come to make inquiries of Adriana Booth. We were told she is the mistress of this manor."

"Come in, sirs. The butler stepped aside to admit them. "I shall inform Mr. Kernley." The butler directed them to the library and disappeared.

The room was richly and tastefully decorated. Plush leather chairs sat comfortably in front of a huge fireplace and bright sunlight filled the room, reflecting off the rich dark wood paneling. Books filled the shelves lining two walls and bespoke the erudition of the residents. This was a man's room, Robert thought, his opinion reinforced by the medical texts that dominated several of the shelves. Adriana's father, of course.

Robert's musings were interrupted by approaching footsteps. A small, lean man entered. He wore glasses, which gave his face a rather pinched air that was heightened by his pallor. This was not a man who spent any time absorbing what there was of the English sunshine.

"Good afternoon, gentlemen. I am Paul Kernley, Miss Booth's solicitor. I understand you have come to call on her, but she is not in residence at this time. Is there some service I can provide?" Robert instantly felt this man was one to be trusted.

Kernley directed them to chairs and called for tea. Once they were settled, Paul looked at both men with anticipation.

"Mr. Kernley, we have come with questions about Adriana. I fear for her safety."

Kernley knitted his brow. "And who are you to her? And why do you think she is at risk?" The man was suddenly agitated and his voice shook.

"I met Adriana on the voyage to the colonies. It is my ship she boarded disguised as an old woman."

Kernley ineffectively suppressed his smile at that. "Was she successful?"

"Quite." This from Tate.

"I fell in love with her and fully intend to make her my wife," Robert continued.

Kernley looked at him oddly and Tate laughed. "The captain means he fell in love with her without the disguise."

Robert gave him a quelling look and Tate had the good grace to drop his gaze.

"Did you know her stepmother was trying to kill her. She shot at her and Adriana bears the scar on her shoulder."

"I know someone fired at her, luckily only striking

her shoulder. We decided it might be a good choice for her to go away for a while." He grinned. "The disguise was her idea and I am pleased to hear it worked. No one recognized her."

"Someone did," Robert stated flatly. "Would her stepmother have been the one to shoot her? It is my understanding she had a motive."

Kernley shook his head. "I happen to know Sarah Jane was terrified of guns. I do know she had no love lost for her stepdaughter, but she would not shoot her. Perhaps poison or some other method would make sense. But she certainly might have hired someone who was happily a bad aim. But it could not be proven."

"Or perhaps it was her childhood friend Jason? To frighten Adriana into needing his protection. He was the one to follow her to Virginia."

"I hate to say it, but now that you give voice to it, it does make sense. About Jason, I mean. It makes me ill to think of it." Frowning in concentration, he suddenly looked up. "He did come by here, and I mentioned to him that Adriana had gone away for a short time. It didn't occur to me at the time that he was responsible." He heaved a sigh. "This is all my fault. I should have told him she was merely visiting relatives nearby."

"No. You had no way of knowing he was a threat and you said nothing untoward. The man is a nightmare."

"Tell me what happened," the lawyer prompted. "And where you believe Adriana is now. You must think she is returning home or you would not be here."

"Adriana and I were actually planning our future when the man, Jason, appeared, claiming to be her husband." Speaking the man's name tasted bitter on Robert's tongue. "He showed me documents to verify his claim. I was convinced they were forged, but he said they had a disagreement and she fled from him."

"None of that is true. Why Jason was naught to her but a childhood friend. I am sure he would have liked it to be otherwise. He was clearly smitten with her."

"I fear he has forced her onto a ship sailing back and intends to actually try and compel her to wed. I have given it much thought and it makes sense. That way, he could claim ownership of her estate."

"That is beneath contempt," Paul sneered.

"There is more. A slight complication if that is his plan. He was married to another whilst he was in Virginia."

"Then Adriana is safe from being coerced into taking vows."

"Unless the miscreant has plans to rid himself of his current wife, who has much wealth of her own."

A woman appeared at the door carrying a tray with tea, cups, and some delicate pastries. She discreetly walked to a low table and deposited the service and moved to leave the room. Suddenly, she faced Paul. "Sorry, sir, but I cannot wait another minute to ask. I could not help but overhear you and these men have been discussing Miss Adriana." Turning to face Robert, anxiety colored her cheeks. " Is she well? Is she coming home? I miss her terribly."

Paul pasted on a smile and turned to his guests. "Cassie is the family cook and has been a second mother to Adriana since her own died."

Cassie was in her thirties and very pretty, with delicate features and a lovely mouth. Her skin was smooth, but her blue eyes were wide with worry.

"Why, she is certainly not old enough to be Adriana's mother," Tate commented.

Cassie blushed more deeply at the compliment. "We spent a great deal of time together after her mother so tragically passed. I taught her to cook."

"You are the blessed angel who gave her such skill. You are to be praised."

Smiling at the two, Paul interrupted their exchange. "Cassie, I promise to fill you in on each and every detail as soon as our business is concluded. Miss Adriana will, hopefully, be coming home soon."

"Yes, we will see to it," Tate stated.

Cassie gave him a dazzling smile and Tate suddenly took on the appearance of a lovesick puppy. Robert raised his eyebrows at the man he thought he knew so well. He never expected Tate to be so taken with a female. It was certainly not that he did not appreciate women. It was more he always said he did not have time to include them in his life. Until, it seemed, recently.

"Oh, thank you so much, sir. I shall wait until you gentlemen have finished." She took her leave after one more glance at Tate, who by now seemed totally distracted.

Paul poured some tea for himself and his guests. He sipped the steaming liquid, his expression thoughtful. "Did you manage to make the journey here ahead of him?"

"I am certain of that. No ship is faster than the Windstar."

Robert was in no mood for tea. "Can you tell us the details of her choosing to leave here?"

"Adriana came to see me soon after she healed from her wound. As I said, we decided she should travel away from her home for a time, at least until whoever was responsible for hurting her was found. She asked me to oversee the management of her estate while she was away and I was happy to oblige. I have served her family as solicitor since before she was born. Everyone knew she grieved for her father and it made sense she might need some time away."

"So you both conceived the idea of a disguise?"

His hand shaking and rattling the cup, he attempted another sip of tea. "Yes. We thought ourselves very clever. Obviously not clever enough. I never even thought to worry since I had no expectation of hearing from her for months. But now that I know what actually happened, Jason's motives have more than raised my apprehension. What would have persuaded him to follow her across the sea unless to coerce her in some way? Adriana made it clear she had no interest in him for anything more than friendship. Although, I do believe she suspected he was not the open hearted boy from her youth." Paul lowered his voice, as if disclosing an intimacy. "I do not like to discuss anything that I cannot verify, but there were nasty rumors in regard to his late wife."

"He was married before?"

"Now, I am certainly not one to gossip, but there was talk that his wife died before her time if you get my meaning. And his parents… well, they died in a brutal assault with an axe. He was cleared of guilt, but no one ever felt sure of his innocence."

"You are saying he is a murderer? Her very life could be at risk?" Robert felt his heart stop and leave his body. After a moment, he felt it had returned and now, it was pounding so hard, it threatened to fly again. He struggled for composure.

"Yes, I suppose I am. But Adriana will certainly be wary of him. And she is well known here. He dare not harm her.

Robert's throat nearly closed with dread and guilt.

"It does worry me that he went to so much trouble to concoct this story of marriage. He must be desperate to see her wealth under his control and marriage would be the simplest solution." Which meant he needed her alive. The thought was reassuring. "I never should have left her vulnerable. I should have known after he came to see me that he was a threat. Do you have any idea where Jason might take her?"

"Why to his home, of course. Though it has fallen into the hands of neglect and parts of it have crumbled, it is still mostly intact. No one travels near it, since they fear the ghosts of his dead parents still haunt the place. The English can be a superstitious lot. Jason could take her there and remain undiscovered."

"Where is this place?" Robert asked.

"A quarter mile west. The house sits alone and rather forlorn in the midst of a clearing. You will certainly recognize it when you come upon it. If I hear any word, I shall inform you immediately."

"I thank you. We are staying at the Whispering Beggar."

"By no means. I will have your things sent for and you must lodge here, certainly until Adriana is located and found to be unmolested."

"Thank you for the offer, but it would be more expedient for us to stay near the docks. As I said, I am certain we arrived ahead of the ship carrying Adriana and we need to watch for its approach."

"You will send word when she is safe?" Kernley asked.

"Of course. We will bring her home."

Robert and Tate took their leave and rode swiftly away from the manor house, the beauty of the landscape wasted now on their unmindful eyes.

Chapter Twenty-Nine

Adriana had kept track of the days and knew the journey was coming to an end. Her only comfort was the quickening of the child and she prayed constantly for his safety.

She was unsure of Jason's plan once they arrived in England. Maybe he could be tricked into confiding in her. Certainly, if he thought it would unnerve her, he would expose his strategies. Hadn't he done just that in her cottage? The first few times she had broached the subject Jason glared at her or laughed in her face. This morning, however, he seemed to be in a different frame of mind.

"Good morning, Adriana. How are you this fine day?"

"Good morning, Jason. I would greet the sun if it were visible."

"Well, my dear, it cannot be helped. We shall reach our destination before too many more days have passed, so you can look forward to improved accommodations."

"Why?" The word flew from her mouth before she thought about it. The question had plagued her for so long now. "Why are you doing this? Is it just for my money?"

"Why? Why are you here? Why do I want you? Why am I the way I am? Which 'why' do you seek an answer for?"

"All of them, I suppose." Defeat was wearing on her.

Jason leaned against the wall next to the door, stretched out his legs and crossed his arms over his chest. "Well, today it might just amuse me to give you some answers. Naught could be harmed by it. All right, I shall tell you a story. Once upon a time there lived a man and his wife and their young son. The man had a mean streak and a wicked temper, and the woman was his match. It seemed they had a child by accident, never having the inclination to actually care for anyone but themselves. At some point, it must have occurred to them that the boy could be useful, so they sent him to play with the little girl whose family lived in the large manor not too far away. The little boy was taught what he must do and each time he came home from a visit, he bore a gift of some sort. Candlesticks, silverware, anything deemed to have value. If, on the rare occasion, he returned empty-handed, the parents took turns beating him and reminding him of his worthlessness. He learned that the only insulation was to have wealth, for the little girl was never beaten. He longed to stay with her and never return to his own parents. At the end of the day, she would wave goodbye and he would be forced to sneak back into the manor to acquire something before his trip home.

"He began to hate the little girl. He knew she could have done something to help him, but she never interceded. He vowed that one day the worm would turn and she would be the one suffering without mercy."

Adriana had listened and her mouth parted in an 'o' of sympathy. "Oh, Jason, I had no idea. If I had, I would have certainly had my parents try to help."

Jason smiled bitterly. "You say that now. Even if that were true, it is way past time. I found I had more inner

180

resources than I ever imagined and I have succeeded without your intercession.

"After the shooting, when I came to call and Kernley said you had gone away to grieve, it made sense you would run to sea. All that was left was to find out which vessel and, therefore, what destination. You know, many a man will tell you all he can for just one more mug of ale or a coin or two. The tale of an old, one-eyed woman appearing one day at the inn and asking so many questions seemed odd to those who frequented the docks. The woman ultimately boarded a ship for the colonies. I knew it was you and your pathetic attempt at a disguise. Once I reached Virginia, why there you were. So I watched and bided my time. Soon enough I was informed of a young widow who recently arrived and then finding your new home was not even a challenge. In fact, I encountered no obstacle except perhaps that stupid little boy who almost ran over me with his horse. If I had not jumped aside when I did, I might have sustained injuries."

"Brian? So you were the one who caused him to fall from his horse and break his leg?" Her earlier suspicions confirmed that he was the one who had been spying on her, she wished she had been more discerning at the time.

"Is that all that happened to him? A shame. I hoped he would at the very least hit his head. It might have taught him better manners. Sometimes I wonder if it is the money I love or the pursuit of it." He paused for a breath. "All I must do now is marry you. Then, I shall have what is yours. How long you continue to draw breath after that, I have not yet decided. I fully intend to use your body as soon as it has rid itself of the brat you carry. If you please me, your life might be extended. Until I tire of you or have spent your money. Then, of course, I must move on.

You do understand?" Did he honestly believe he sounded like someone who was in his right mind?

Adriana gaped at him in disbelief as he talked on. "I will leave this ship with my wife. Or, rather, with a woman who shall step in and take her place, if you get my drift. You see, no one saw me bring you aboard. Worry not, my sweet. Soon we shall be bound in matrimony and all will be well."

Adriana lowered her head and watched the tears drop onto her now-filthy dress. Before she could say more, he was gone, the door locking behind him. She was bereft. If she could not reason with him, there was no hope. If he would not confide his plans, she would not be able to decide how to counter them.

Chapter Thirty

Adriana knew they had reached port when she felt the shifting of the vessel and the groaning of the heavy ropes being tossed to shore. She must try and remain calm and devise a strategy of her own.

She was not without friends here. Her home could offer sanctuary. How silly she had been to take Jason's word and flee from the one place she would have been secure. So many mistakes, so many misjudgments. But then, she never would have met Robert, the love of her life. If only she had the chance to see him once more. And the babe. The child would be the legacy of her love for the handsome captain and she would do whatever it took to keep him safe.

Late in the morning, Jason unlocked the door and entered the cabin that had been her home for so many weeks. He carried a dress and a dark cloak, which he threw at her feet. She recognized it as clothing Melanie had worn and met the icy glare he directed at her. He unlocked her chain and she rubbed the bloody ankle, knowing the marks would never fade.

"Put these clothes on. At least they are clean and do not smell."

"Those belong to Melanie."

He laughed, the sound harsh in the tiny area. "Did belong to Melanie. She has no need of them now."

The thought of donning Melanie's clothes made a shiver run up her spine. "The gown will not fit. She was a larger woman."

"Did you not notice how your middle has stretched? The brat has ruined your tiny waist. Put on the dress. It will help mask your horrible condition. There is no need to confuse the issue with the knowledge you carry a bastard."

She smiled to herself. "But, Jason, no one will ever know it is not your child. Why, when the child is born, you can claim him as your own. There is no greater honor than to sire an heir." She prayed her words would grant her some time.

"Why in the name of God would I need an heir? Trust me, I plan to leave naught behind for another to enjoy. Now, put on the dress and give me no more argument. My patience grows thin and I will see you struck in the stomach should you give me more trouble."

Adriana dropped her head in obedience and unfastened her filthy dress. He stood, staring, and she raised her eyes to catch his gaze. "May I at least have some privacy?"

"Certainly, my lady. Your misshapen body holds no interest for me. I shall grant you five minutes to be suitably clothed before we disembark. See that the hood of the cloak is drawn down sufficiently to cover your hair and face. I want no one to make a distinction between you and my late wife. I warn you now, any attempt to call for aid or even suggest you are anything but totally content in my company will result in most unpleasant circumstances. Do I make myself clear?"

"Yes, my lord." Certain he meant every word of his threat, she decided to acquiesce.

"Good. I like an obedient woman. You might learn

184

yet." Rubbing his hands together with self-satisfaction, he managed a smile that reminded Adriana of depictions of the devil.

Slipping off the old gown and, attempting not to cringe, she stepped into the dress that had once been worn by another. It was overlarge, but no matter. She had no desire to appeal to any man save one and she hoped he was somewhere at sea, pursuing her. Unless he decided that Jason's tale was true. Could Robert have abandoned her? The thought was too horrible to even contemplate.

Wrapping the cloak around her shoulders, she pulled the hood low. She could not help but remember another ship and another disguise such as this. Robert, please. Come for me. I love you so. And even if you no longer care for me, please save me for the sake of your child.

Chapter Thirty-One

The residence the Hadleys had called home showed the result of years of neglect. In sections, the roof had caved in or completely disappeared. Sunlight burst through as if to announce its supremacy. The floors and walls were decorated with mud and vines and all manner of creatures skittered about as Robert's footsteps echoed through the barren space. Once, large fireplaces had occupied either end of the home, but now their bricks fell in a confused pile, as if someone had tried to put them in order and failed.

A staircase led to a second story, but Robert feared the risers would collapse under his weight. All in all, it was the perfect place to hide someone. It was also the ideal place to lie in wait for a villain who expected no such greeting.

Robert and Tate had stopped on their way back to the docks to explore the old ruin, and now Robert took up residence with Tate at the Whispering Beggar where they could keep watch on the comings and goings of the waterfront. They had sailed just a day after Jason and Robert had no doubt they had been faster.

As luck would have it, a new ship was dropping anchor a distance away, but something about it made Robert suspicious. It was a clearly a luxurious vehicle, designed more for passengers than cargo. Robert watched covertly. He wondered if Adriana was hidden in one of the cabins. God, he missed her.

As it settled itself and was tied down, the crew began to disembark onto a rowboat. Oddly, no passengers left the ship. Jason would want no witnesses to his misdeeds, so he would wait until most of the men were gone before leaving the vessel.

When it appeared the ship was empty except for a skeleton crew and Robert was berating himself for his flawed instincts, two figures appeared on deck. A man and woman descended from the ship onto another small boat and made their way to shore. Even in the faint light of early evening, Robert could see the woman valiantly trying to keep some space between them and the man was roughly holding her in place. She lifted her head and, for just the briefest moment, her hood fell back, exposing her face, before the man shoved it forward again.

Racing for their horses before the small boat reached shore, Robert and Tate galloped to the old Hadley home. Jason would most likely hire a covered carriage, since he would not risk Adriana being seen, and that would give them the advantage of time. Robert prayed his instincts were right. He was sure Jason had nowhere else to go.

Hooves dug in and threw clods of dirt into the air as the two sped onward. At their destination, they dismounted and Tate led the sweating beasts behind the house and out of sight. He rubbed them down as Robert strode inside and sought out the niche next to the fireplace he had discerned on his earlier visit. Then, he waited, holding his breath. He did not have to wait overlong. Before an hour passed, two voices approached the house.

When he finally saw her after so many long weeks, Robert was beyond elated. She appeared tired and the

187

child she carried was certainly more prominent, but she was the most beautiful woman he had ever seen. Relief that she was seemingly unharmed quelled the terrible fear that had beset him since he discovered her missing so long ago.

Jason's voice cut into his joy at having her so near. "You have never had the pleasure of seeing my home, have you, my love?"

"No. And I am not your love. You need not continue the pretense."

"But I do love you, Adriana. I always have. Even when I hated you."

When Robert heard Jason speak, his entire body tensed and his blood throttled hard through his veins. He ached to rush out and kill the man with his bare hands, but that might put his beloved at risk. *Patience. Wait until the time is right.*

"What is your intention, now?" demanded Adriana.

"Well, first to welcome you to my home, of course."

"Jason, what game do you play?"

"Oh, my sweet, do not dampen my pleasure. I intend to enjoy every moment of my victory."

"This is your idea of victory?"

"Do not poke the sleeping bear. You do not want to see my ire raised."

"Are we to sleep here? What about food?"

Jason sneered at her. "Cease your complaints, woman. I have seen to our needs. I had the inn prepare a basket while we waited for the carriage. And yes, we shall spend the night here. It will not kill you to sleep on a hard floor. After all, you should have become accustomed to it on the voyage."

Robert's rage became a living thing.

"I shall retrieve the food and pay the driver. In the meanwhile, I trust you will behave. I can still send word to have your captain killed and I will take great delight in seeing the end to that babe of yours as soon as it is born. Do not test me. And do not attempt to escape."

"Where would I go?"

"To your own home, perhaps? But, burdened as you are with the extra weight around your middle, be assured I will catch you and you will not like the result. You can still stand for vows with a broken limb. Or perhaps I shall merely crush your fingers."

A ray of fading sunlight washed Jason's face and Robert could see the other man smiled at Adriana's obvious horror. Jason left her and Robert slipped out from the darkened space. Her eyes grew wide as saucers at the sight of him, her lips lifting with a smile that said how overjoyed she was to see him. He put his index finger to his lips. Then, he held up his hands, palms out, to indicate she should remain where she was and she nodded. He eased back into the shadows and was swallowed by the darkness.

Adriana composed herself. She hoped the blush of joy that was surely on her cheeks would not be visible in the semi-darkness as Jason re-entered the room.

Dropping a wicker basket on the floor, he looked at her with disdain. "There is your nourishment. Sustain yourself for come the morrow you will be my bride."

She stepped back, out of his reach and pretended to approach the food from the opposite side. His gaze followed her as she directed his line of sight away from where Robert stood, so when Robert spoke from behind him, he nearly jumped out of his skin. "No, Hadley. Not *your* bride. Only mine."

***

The men were on each other like rabid animals. Jason produced a blade and swung viciously at Robert, who dodged the strike. The metal caught the light of the moon and glinted its threat. Adriana backed against the wall, her palms pressing the bricks. She desperately wanted to jump in and stop this battle, but she knew she would merely make the situation worse. She had to have faith in the man she loved.

Robert was taller and stronger, but Jason was wiry and determined. Their muscles stood out in vivid relief as they danced and feinted, moved in and circled. Adriana could barely breathe and could only pray.

She was startled when someone grasped her arm. She nearly screamed before she realized it was Tate. She begged without words for him to help. He just smiled and leaned against the wall next to her, as casually as if he were watching a Sunday stroll in the park. He rubbed her arm to let her know the captain had this matter in hand.

After what seemed like an eternity, Jason's knife clattered to the stone floor. Jason threw himself forward, landing on the ground by the knife and grabbing it. Then he was back up on his feet, turning to Robert, but Robert grabbed hold of his wrist and twisted it back on itself. The blade found its sheath in Jason's chest and the air whooshed out of him. He fell to his knees, then to his back and lay still. Blood flowed from the gaping wound onto the floor. The battle was done. Suddenly, there was a deathly silence in the room. For a moment, no one moved.

Robert leaned down and checked the limp man. Satisfied he was dead, he stood and ran to Adriana who fairly jumped into his arms. He kissed her mouth, her cheeks as his lips drank away the tears of relief running down her face. She hugged him as hard as she could, her emotions overwhelming. She felt so much relief and love and gratitude. "You saved me."

"Of course. Did you expect any less of me? I had to rescue the woman I love." Robert turned to Tate. "By the by, you were a huge help."

Tate laughed. "I do believe you are bleeding, captain," The stain of red stood in vivid relief against his coat. A line of gore had made a path from his wrist to his hand and dripped to the ground.

"Oh, my God," Adriana gasped.

"It is nothing. A scratch. And I have it on good authority you have some skill as a doctor."

"Then, let me tend it."

"Later. I assure you, it is not worth your time at the moment."

Adriana gave him a quelling look. She had every intention of caring for him as soon as they were gone from this place. Then, she looked over at the lifeless man sprawled on the floor. "Is he dead?"

"It appears so."

Apprehension creased her brow. "Cinnamon and Blossom? I had to leave them and I hoped you would see to their care."

"They are both safe and well and the only worry now is that my mother may never let you take the pup back."

Adriana laughed, the joy from relief. "I want to go home."

"Yes, my love." He turned to Tate. "Can you see to the man's burial? Just get some of the crew and they will oblige, I am sure. Not that he deserves any kind of honor, but it is the right thing to do. Then, please release them from duty, secure the ship and join us at the manor. We shall spend the winter here."

"The men?" Adriana gasped. "One of your men is a traitor and means to kill you. Jason told me he had an assassin on board your vessel. You must root out the man before he can do you injury."

Robert laughed aloud. "Adriana, I have known each member of my crew for years, each and every one. A stranger could not just come aboard my ship."

"Unless she was an old woman who could cook," Tate interjected.

Robert glared at him. "Jason was exaggerating the facts, I am sure, to keep you in check. I am just so relieved you are safe and in one piece. If a bit dirty."

"It is good to see you again, Miss Adriana," Tate piped up.

She smiled. "You, too, Tate. Thank you for coming to my aid."

"Why thank him?" Robert asked, his chest puffing up. "I was your champion."

She laughed out loud. "Yes," she said, a bit patronizing. "You were indeed my savior. And I shall be eternally grateful."

"Really? Would you then grant me a small favor in return?"

She eyed him suspiciously. "What kind of *small* favor?"

"Would you agree to marry me as soon as I can arrange it?"

She was delighted but kept it in check. "Well, if I must."

"Oh, I insist."

"I love a man who knows his own mind."

"Is there anything I can do for you this day, my lady, besides save you?" He was leering at her.

She nodded her head with enthusiasm. "Yes, my love. Food. And a bath. Since it has recently been brought to my attention that I am *dirty*. And some clean clothes."

"Not exactly the requests I was hoping for."

"No doubt.

Chapter Thirty-Two

"Miss Adriana. Praise God," the butler cried. When he saw them, his eyes widened with delight. "Cassie, Martha, Mr. Kernley, come quickly. It is Miss Adriana. She is home." He looked directly at her. "You are well, are you not?" His eyes dipped to her abdomen and his left eyebrow raised slightly.

She laughed out loud. "Yes, George, I am indeed well." Before she could speak another word, she was crushed in the embraces of Martha, Cassie, and Paul. After holding her for dear life, Martha stepped back and sniffed the air. "What is that smell? And what happened?" Everyone was looking at her middle.

"I believe that odor issues from me. Long weeks on a ship without washing will leave its mark. Can I please get a bath? And then I will tell you all of my adventures. But first, I require some water and bandages. The captain, here, sustained an injury defending me and we must tend it."

Martha and Cassie scurried away while Paul ushered Robert into the library. "You do look a little the worse for wear yourself, Captain. I can only surmise from your appearance that you have rid the world of the threat to Adriana. And so quickly. I am impressed."

"You are astute, Paul. It was not pretty, but it is done." Cassie appeared at the library door and looked about expectantly. Robert turned and smiled at her. "Tate has gone to see to some arrangements and should be arriving soon."

Cassie blushed at this information, having believed herself to be more subtle than she was. "Oh, I was just coming to see if you required anything."

"My guess is he could do with some brandy," Paul suggested. Robert nodded his approval.

Adriana swept into the room with a basin and white bandages and bid Robert remove his coat. The wound, as he had said, was not deep and was quickly dispatched with some careful washing and wraps.

"I believe you will live," Adriana pronounced, her ministerings complete.

"That is good news. But, my love, I must say, the odor that issues from you might be the death of me. Can you see to that?"

She puffed herself up in feigned righteous indignation and left the room, his laughter echoing behind her. "Pretty haughty for such smelly baggage," he called out, his amusement still evident.

The two men sat and Robert told of the events transpiring since they had left the manor. Cassie brought tea, and snifters of brandy and left the men alone.

"Such a stroke of luck that you saw them disembark," Paul said.

"It was a miracle."

***

Adriana stepped into the warmth of the tub. Suddenly, the tears flowed in earnest. It was like opening a floodgate. Martha ran to her and stroked her hair, then applied soap to the greasy mass and worked the suds through it. She rinsed the tresses and scrubbed her mistress's back, allowing Adriana to sob out the misery as Martha rubbed her shoulders to offer comfort.

Finally, the agony eased and Adriana dipped her hands into the water and washed her face. Her breathing remained hitched, but she was calmer.

"Can you speak of it, angel? It will help if you can tell me."

Adriana nodded and slowly, in bits, the story spun out. Martha kept interjecting with things like "Jason! I cannot believe it" and "Dear Lord" and "I never would have trusted you with him if I had but thought" and "you cooked for an entire crew"?" Finally, the tale was done and Adriana was spent.

Martha helped her from the tub and was reaching for a towel. "Miss Adriana, have you perchance left something out in your recounting?"

Adriana realized Martha was looking at her waist, now much rounder than before she left. Adriana felt her color rise. "Oh, yes. I did forget to tell you about him."

"Him?"

"I am quite convinced it is a boy. I hope he looks exactly like his father."

"Who is—the captain I am guessing? How did this happen?" Martha asked.

"I believe the usual way. It was the last night on the voyage and I had merely shed my masquerade for a few moments. He was a bit... full of drink and... well, the details are unimportant." She was embarrassed and could not tell how wanton she had been that night.

Martha huffed her outrage. "And he has not married you? I will not see your child come into this world as a bastard."

"He will marry me," Adriana soothed. "Maybe even this day. It was difficult to plan my nuptials when I smelled like a goat."

Satisfied, Martha chose a soft velvet gown of emerald-green for Adriana, high-waisted and generously cut. It highlighted her eyes. Martha combed the thick, blonde tresses until they were dry and gleamed in the light pouring through the bedroom window. She twisted the mass into an elaborate coiffure, with curls surrounding Adriana's cheeks.

Adriana savored feeling like a lady again. The softness of the gown and the silkiness of the chemise beneath soothed her and, with the future she had dreamed of before her, she was elated.

Chapter Thirty-Three

The church was small and rustic, comfortably settled between an ancient graveyard and a lovely flower garden. The small group approached the doors, which were swung wide by Father Spooner, a man who did not look the part of a village priest. Where one might expect a full profile and round cheeks, he was narrow of body and face, with a long, hooked nose. He might have appeared very stern if not for his eyes, full of warmth and welcome. They had decided on a discreet ceremony which could be accomplished quickly, since Adriana and Robert were both anxious to marry as soon as possible. Adriana was worried that Elizabeth would be hurt to have missed the nuptials, but Robert assured her that their happiness was everything to his mother and she would understand.

Earlier, while Adriana was bathing, Robert had ridden back to Windstar to collect some clothes and see to the business of his ship. Tate had approached him, the look on his face warning of bad news.

"I sent some boys to collect the body and bury it, but it was gone, Captain."

"Gone? Then, he was not dead after all? But I checked his breathing and would swear he was dead."

"Maybe he held his breath. I only know he was not there. Could someone have taken the corpse away?"

"I suppose it is possible. But who would have a reason to do such a thing? None of this makes sense. Well, for now, say naught to Adriana. We must be ever vigilant, to see that no harm comes to her. If he still lives, he will be more desperate than ever and that will make him more dangerous."

"Agreed."

"Change your clothes, man. You have a wedding to attend this day."

"Aye, Captain. It shall be my pleasure. And none too soon. I was afraid your son would have to be best man."

They stood before Father Spooner. Robert had dressed in a deep blue silk waistcoat that matched his breeches. He wore a coat in a darker blue hue, embroidered with gold threads that formed an elaborate pattern down the front and at the cuffs. His white shirt was edged with lace with a jabot at his throat that complemented his sun-darkened skin. Adriana had never seen a more handsome man as she walked toward him.

Adriana had chosen a dress of pale blue silk, full skirted with seed pearls around the square neckline and sleeves. Her hair had been fashionably coifed into ringlets swept atop her head and cascading down her back. Ribbons with more pearls were intricately woven into her curls. Pure joy sparkled in her eyes as she approached the priest and Robert's intake of breath made her smile with satisfaction. Even with a swollen middle, she knew he found her beautiful and she knew this was the happiest moment of her life. She would cherish this time in her memory forever.

The Father's eyes wandered to her waistline. She hoped he did not judge them. Obviously, they were marrying a bit later than was proper.

Robert, Adriana, Tate, Paul, George, Cassie, and Martha clustered around the couple as the holy man reached for his bible. Vows were said and blessings done. The Father called for the ring and Tate, grinning like a fool, produced a wide gold band. The priest blessed it and handed to Robert, who slipped it on Adriana's finger.

All too quickly, the ritual was complete. Robert kissed her with such passion Adriana feared they would embarrass the entire company.

As they signed the necessary documents, Robert laughed.

"What amuses you—husband?"

"These papers. They look nothing like the ones Jason produced. He must not have paid too much for his forgeries."

"Well, these are real. And these are forever."

"Yes, Adriana. Forever."

Chapter Thirty-Four

As the sky stained with the vibrant colors of sunset, they sat down to dinner. At one point, Tate rose with a glass in his hand. "To the most beautiful bride and the luckiest groom."

Robert stood also. "Tate. We have a gift for you." He cleared his throat, addressing the company. "Let me just say that, after so many years of *discretion* and *loyal* service, he is entitled to a reward. So, my wife," he said, grinning down at her, "and I have decided to present him with a home of his own. We were hoping Adriana's cottage would be suitable." He turned to Adriana. "Since it was purchased by my wife originally, between us we must determine a fair price and I shall settle with you. Or perhaps we should negotiate in a more private place to see the terms are amenable." He leered at her and she blushed scarlet.

Tate's jaw dropped, his mouth agape. "Sir, I—"

"No words necessary." The two men toasted each other.

***

After they had eaten until they could hold no more, the newlyweds pleaded exhaustion and retired upstairs to their bedroom. The hearth blazed with warmth and the candles shed soft light about the room. He closed the portal behind him. "I have one question, my love. What of the babe?" Worry creased lines between his eyes.

Adriana raised her eyebrows. "The babe?"

He grinned. "My intention is to fully consummate our union this night, but I do not wish harm to come to my child."

"Oh, your son is a tough one. He has survived much these last months and I feel sure a night of love, shared carefully, will do him no damage."

"If you are certain. I fear I cannot limit myself to just one night."

"Then we shall continue to make attempts until I am so big you cannot reach the parts you seek." She giggled, but the sound was stifled as he placed his lips on hers. First, he was very careful, as though she were made of some fragile material, but when she returned his passion measure for measure, he relaxed and became more demanding.

At one point, he abruptly stopped kissing her and held her, tight, against his chest. He inhaled her intoxicating fragrance. "I have waited so long," he breathed. Then, easing his hold, his lips met hers again. He threw off his coat and swept her into his arms. He carried her to the welcoming softness of the bed.

First, he undid the coils of her hair, spreading the thick blonde length out across the coverlet like an angel's wings. Just looking at her fanned the fires of his lust. His manhood tightened with a life all its own. He unfastened her gown and pulled it down to expose the silk chemise. Desire roared through him like a torrent. He threw the dress to the floor and slid the undergarment over her head, then lowered his eyes to drink in every detail of her lush curves. He reverently stroked her abdomen, feeling the pulse of life there. His gaze raised to her full breasts, the pink hued tips standing impudently, demanding his attention. God, she was magnificent. Robert moved his hand first over one, teasing the peak, then the other. After a moment, his lips replaced his fingers. The tips grew harder still.

Adriana groaned and eased back so she could unfasten his waistcoat. Then, with agonizing slowness, she unbuttoned his white shirt, exposing the skin stretching across the muscles of his chest. She moved her mouth to taste him. It was sweet torment as she reached to unfasten his now over-tight breeches. His manhood sprung free, desperately eager.

Unable to control himself longer, he pushed her back into the soft bed and carefully lowered himself on top of her, his manhood insistent against the velvet skin of her thigh. He slid inside her, savoring the moist heat. He held fast for a moment. She wrapped her fingers into his hair, pulling his mouth to hers and kissing him hard, demanding. She parted his lips with her tongue and explored his mouth. He could no longer contain the conflagration boiling in his loins. He thrust forward, then pulled back, only to plunge forward yet again. They moved as one until their passion exploded, bathing them both in the white light of contentment.

Slowly they floated back, secure in each other's arms, warm and sated.

"You are the most beautiful of brides, my love."

"And you the most handsome groom. I cannot believe we have finally come to this place, this here and now, when for so long I thought it impossible."

"It was indeed a bumpy road. But understand this. I am so in love with you, I feel as if I have been bewitched. Now that I have you, I shall never let you go. We will have many stories with which to regale our grandchildren."

"Grandchildren?" she fairly shrieked, laughing. "Can I have our first child before you relegate me to old age?"

"I plan to have you with me until our children's children are old and gray."

"That is a lovely thought. But, I have to know— what did you think of me that first night we were together? I am quite aware of your inebriated state, but you must have some memory of our encounter."

He laughed. "Some memory? It is all I have thought about since then. Your face, the scent of you, the feel of your body against me. I honestly believed I had lost my senses. This magnificent woman appeared and then was gone. I wondered if some demon had possessed me just to see me suffer with the loss."

"And you did not think I was a… whore?"

"Hardly, my sweet. Whores are not virgins. It is a contradiction in terms."

"Why did you not see through my disguise?"

"Because I am a stupid, blind man. Sometimes, we only look at the surface and fail to look beneath. I claim a flaw in my gender. I can only beg you to forgive my ignorance. I promise to spend the rest of my life making it up to you."

"Well, I might consider forgiving you if you answer one more question."

"Only a wife for a few short hours and already a nag."

She slapped him on the arm. "I am no such thing. I merely want to know."

"Anything. Just ask."

"After I came to your home and saved you from Melanie's lies, you let me go. Except for that one visit which was very unsatisfactory. You did not seek me out or try to apologize or show any care for me at all."

"That is how you see it. The truth is I passed by your cottage at least once each day to catch a glimpse of you. I rode my horse to the top of the crest and watched for you. And I gave you a puppy."

"Tate gave me a puppy."

"Where do you think he got it? I had to pay a pretty penny for that mutt."

"You got Blossom for me?" She was melting.

"It was Tate's idea, actually. He was reluctant to betray your confidence, so he came to me with an idea. He said he might have a witness—someone who could contradict Melanie's claims and send her on her way. But, he needed a bribe."

"You did not think it suspicious that the payment would be a tiny dog?"

"All right, I did not know exactly what he had in mind. The pup was his idea, but I paid for her."

"I miss her and Cinnamon. I worry about them."

"Do not fret. They are well cared for. I saw to it before we sailed.

"When Jason came to you—you never doubted me."

"No."

"That is amazing. Why did you trust me?"

"I suppose I knew your nature. It was that woman I fell in love with. Old, young, it was always you. Isn't that true love?"

"I am the luckiest woman alive."

Chapter Thirty-Five

The time flew by. Tate appeared to be a new man. Robert noticed his normally gruff manner softening. Each time Cassie appeared, Tate dissolved into a stammering mess and Cassie blushed a becoming bright red. Everyone pretended not to notice how the two were becoming nearly inseparable. No one wanted to embarrass them in their growing affection for each other, but all hoped for an announcement soon.

To everyone's joy and relief, in the late autumn, a lovely ruby ring graced Cassie's left hand, and soon after, Father Spooner was called upon yet again to perform his duties. This time, Robert and Adriana stood as witnesses for the couple.

They spent time arranging for their departure come early spring, after the birth. Paul was to remain at Bereston and see to its continued good condition. Cassie, of course, would be leaving with Tate for Virginia. Her cooking became extravagant. Her joy was expressed in the kitchens and all benefited. In fact, the men complained that they were looking more like Adriana, with their expanding waistlines.

Tate talked of his new home and drew plans for Cassie, saying how they would need to expand the kitchen, of course.

The only distraction from the happiness for Robert was the gnawing fear that Jason might re-appear. His body was never found and inquiries into his possible whereabouts yielded naught. Still, he did not confide his concerns to Adriana, feeling it was unnecessary to upset her, especially now that her condition was becoming advanced.

"What is it?" Adriana demanded one evening.

"What, my love?"

"What troubles you so? And do not bother to lie to me."

"There is nothing…"

"I am certain I just told you not to lie to me."

He nodded his head in resignation. "It is Jason."

"Jason? Is he not dead and buried? Why would he worry you?"

"I am unsure if he is actually dead."

"What? But you killed him. I watched him die. We watched him die."

"So we thought. But when I sent men to bury his body, he had disappeared. I worry that I might have been mistaken and he still lives."

"So, he may yet be a threat?"

"I think not. Not to you, anyway. His goal was to make you his bride and claim your fortune. There is no possible way for him to accomplish that now."

Adriana suddenly was cold as ice. A shiver ran up her spine and she hesitated to give voice to the thought that chilled her so. "Unless—he killed you." This came out in a choked whisper.

Robert grinned at her. "He will not kill me. I bested him before and I would do so again if the situation presented. He is a coward. His prey are women and the helpless. You will not rid yourself of me quite so easily as that."

"Oh, Robert, do not jest." She threw herself into his arms. He held her as closely as the growing child would allow and stroked her hair until she calmed.

"Why did you not tell me sooner?"

"And upset you—to what end? Perhaps upset the babe, as well. I will take care of this. You have my word. Do not lose a moment's rest over this. Do you trust me?"

"Yes, of course. But, I love you so much. I do not know what I would do without you."

"Then, do not think on it, since it will never come to pass that I will leave you."

That night, as she lay in her bed, Jason suddenly loomed above her and grabbed her arm. He covered her mouth so she could not scream. Robert lay beside her, deeply asleep or—perish the thought—dead, as she was dragged away, desperate to not give in to her terror. She wanted to scream at Robert to awaken him—Robert, you promised, you promised—but the words were trapped in her throat. With horror, she glanced back at her husband. On top of the lacy coverlet, he laid in a pool of his own blood. He did not come to her aid because he could not. Jason had killed him.

She had been taken aboard the same ship that had brought her back to England, in that terrible cabin. Her baby was here, too, crying, in pain, screaming for her, but she could not see him. Adriana could not help him.

Jason again stood over her with a knife. Behind him, the watery image of Melanie narrowed its eyes. "This is all your fault," she banshee cried. Terror nearly stopped her heart as Jason's blade swung down toward her, whistling its threat as it came close. "No," she screamed.

Suddenly, Adriana was wrapped in Robert's strong arms. He was rocking her and she was back home in her bed, safe. She could barely breathe.

"You were dreaming, love. It must have been a terrible nightmare. But you are safe. No one will harm you."

"Oh, Robert, he kidnapped me again and threatened our child. I was trapped. You could not help me or the babe. You were dead—he killed you—you lay there in your own blood. It was horrible," she sobbed.

"The things you fear are not real. I will always be here. I told you that and I meant it. Rest now, sweet." He held her against his body and whispered soft words until she relaxed slightly, the terrible images fading.

Chapter Thirty-Six

One evening in November, when the world was turning cold, preparing for the onslaught of winter, Adriana decided to bathe after supper. She had been full of energy all day and had been bustling about the manor straightening this and rearranging that. She heard Martha tell Cassie she was nesting and alerted Cassie to be ready for the appearance of a new life.

Adriana was just rising from the steaming tub when Robert strolled into the room. At the sight of her, he halted and issued a low whistle of appreciation.

"Oh, please, Robert. I look like a whale. I have not seen my toes in weeks. I cannot get comfortable, no matter the position I attempt. This son of yours grows heavier every day. I want nothing more than to hold him in my arms."

"You are glorious with my child held safe within your body. I have never seen you more beautiful."

"I do believe you imbibed too much wine at dinner, since your vision is obviously affected."

He moved toward her, as if stalking prey. She pushed her hands forward, to discourage his game and the linen towel fell into the bathwater. "Now look what you have done with your lusty ways."

"That is nothing to what I intend, my delicious little morsel." He rubbed his hands together and cackled at her.

210

"Oh." Bending over, she breathed in quick gasps as the pain nearly overtook her.

"Oh what? Are you well? Let me help you."

Concerned edged his brow. He wrapped one arm around her waist and guided her out of the tub and toward the bed. Before they could accomplish their intended goal, she leaned forward, grabbing her abdomen. A gush of fetal water coursed down her legs and onto the wooden floor. Robert stared aghast, clearly unsure the meaning of this.

Adriana smiled at him. "I believe it is normal. It is time for your son to join us. Would you summon Martha and Cassie?"

He froze for a moment.

"Robert?"

"Right. Cassie. Martha," he responded, as if he were sleepwalking. He turned to run from the room. He stopped. He whirled on his heel and rushed back to her side, aiding her walk to the bed, now at least five miles away. Once she was comfortable, he ran to the door. "Martha, Cassie!"

Adriana shook her head. "Men. Always so reliable in time of crisis."

***

The pale streaks of dawn had split the dark night sky, painting it with rosy streaks and purple lights when, finally, Adriana's cries ceased. The first lusty cries of a baby rang out.

Robert was pacing, wincing each time her voice raised in pain. When it finally stopped, he did not know whether to panic or be glad. He no longer heard his love.

211

Terror wrapped about his heart like an iron band just as Martha appeared at the door, a smile lighting her face. "You have a boy. And he is a handsome lad."

"Adriana?"

"Tired. But pretty proud of herself. It is not the easiest job to push a babe into this world, but she came through it fine. He is now wrapped in her arms. Would you like to meet your son?"

Robert approached the bed slowly, at first nervous as he looked down at the tiny life. One glance and he fell immediately in love. The baby's perfect features, red from the huge effort of being born, were in repose as he slept on his mother's breast. There was so much love inside Robert that it threatened to burst out in brilliant colors and light the room.

His beautiful wife, cradling their son, had never been more glorious. She glowed with pride and looked at Robert in a way that made him feel like he could climb any mountain, slay any dragon. He was enraptured.

Suddenly, Adam opened his mouth and let out a cry that shook the very rafters. Robert jumped at the sound, laughing. "How could that little thing create such a noise?"

"He is hungry. Like his father, he makes demands and expects them to be met—immediately." She placed her nipple into the babe's mouth.

"Well, by all means, do not keep the lad waiting. One more cry like that and I fear the house will come down around us."

"It is a good sign."

"I know. I am so proud of you. I am so happy." He stroked Adriana's soft cheek.

"As am I."

212

"Who would have thought such an old woman could bear such a strong child?"

"I suppose it is because she was never really old. His father was just too blind to notice."

"But the old woman and the stupid captain managed to create the most handsome child on earth. So, now it must become the thing of stories."

"Oh, I agree it is worthy of a legend. For who would believe the truth?"

"I just have one question."

"Yes, my love?"

"If I cry out, may I have the same reaction as young Adam? Can I feed from your bounty, my lady?"

Adriana shook her head. "Your lust will be the death of me. You must, at least for a short time, control your urges since I need some time to heal."

"Is there aught I can do to speed the process?" He leered at her.

"You are the devil," she laughed.

Chapter Thirty-Seven

A party. Yes! The idea had come to her this morning as she was feeding Adam—already a month old. It was time to celebrate. Adriana was so overcome with joy, she felt it would fair burst from her. She felt like the most blessed among women. She wanted nothing more than to share it with friends.

"I wish to have a celebration," she declared at breakfast.

Her good mood was contagious. The cloud of Jason had hung about, but it moved away as more time passed and he was not in evidence. Tate saw to it that men were always outside the manor keeping a vigil. No one would slip past unnoticed.

"That is a wonderful idea," Robert agreed. "When?"

"Oh, I have not decided. I only thought of the idea. I suppose, the sooner, the better. How about in two weeks?"

"Will there be time for preparations? When my mother had parties, it took her months to plan." He hesitated, then asked if she was recovered sufficiently from the birth.

"I have never been more well and we can manage. Besides, we leave for Virginia soon and I should like to have another celebration there. I will think of this as practice."

Robert burst out laughing. "Whatever my lady desires. So let it be done."

Adriana was in a whirlwind of motion for days. Robert was amused when she jumped up at the first sign of light to tend to Adam. Then, she rushed onward with the arrangements. She changed her mind about the menu four times and Robert worried Cassie might explode from frustration. Finally things settled down as the plans came together.

The night of the event, Adriana was in the bedroom dressing. Robert appeared at the door in his forest green breeches and waistcoat. The devil was in his eyes as he watched her comb her hair. Dressed in but a thin chemise, she sparked his ardor and it was all he could do to keep his hands from her.

"So, tell me, my lady, when do you think it will be time to give our son a playmate?"

She laughed out loud. "Not tonight."

"I see. Well, tell me this. Has your husband thanked you for the child you bore so recently?"

"Thanked me how?"

"You know. As proper husbands are supposed to do. With gifts."

"Hmmm. I have received no such presents. I do believe I deserve one. Pushing Adam into this world was no easy task. Well worth the trouble, though."

"Will this suffice to express my undying gratitude?" Robert held out a red velvet box.

Adriana looked at it, then into his eyes. He could see the excitement radiating from her. She opened the gift and cried out her delight. .A magnificent necklace of gold, sapphires, and diamonds winked in the candlelight. "Oh, Robert, it is gorgeous. Thank you."

"There are no words to tell you how grateful I am for you and Adam. Consider this a small token of my affection."

"I would hate to see a large token—or maybe I would not hate it."

She rose from her seat and turned so Robert could fasten the piece. Then, she wrapped her arms around his neck and kissed him soundly. Touching the necklace, she smiled. "I will treasure it always."

"Madam, if you continue with this behavior, we shall keep our guests waiting for hours."

"You are terrible. Now, go away and let me finish dressing. I shall properly thank you after the guests have taken their leave."

"Lucky for you, I am a patient man. You are well enough?"

"I am well enough."

He smiled with anticipation and fairly danced from the room.

***

When Adriana appeared at the top of the staircase a bit later, the guests stopped and stared. Her deep blue velvet gown was simple in its cut and emphasized her once again narrow waistline, the low square neckline highlighting her full décolletage. The necklace Robert had just bestowed on her gleamed in the candlelight. She floated down the steps and took her beaming husband by the arm. Together they greeted their company. She was so happy she even dared a sip or two of champagne. The night, the food, the music, and the camaraderie were perfection. Everyone was enjoying themselves.

After an hour, Adriana excused herself to check on Adam. She knew that Martha would see to him if he cried, but she liked looking at him. He was such a lovely boy.

She walked up the stairs and into the nursery. A ray of moonlight spilled through the window and fell on his crib. Adriana was startled to see it empty, but relaxed seeing a woman sitting in the nearby rocker cradling the infant. The woman's head was down, but the hair on Adriana's neck tightened. It wasn't Martha or Cassie holding her child.

Who was rocking her son? When the woman raised her head, Adriana nearly screamed.

"Say nothing, raise no alarm, or I shall drop him," Sarah Jane Booth threatened, her voice never rising above a whisper.

Adriana felt as if all the air was suddenly gone from the room. She reached out to her child, but Sarah Jane shook her head. "Do not move. Do not make me nervous."

"No, no, please, not my son. Please. I beg you. Do what you like to me, but return him to his cradle. I shall do whatever you say."

"Of course you will. Sorry to keep you from your party. I know you think you have so much to celebrate. But, what of me? Have you given no thought to me?"

"Jason told me you were dead. He said he killed you."

"That sounds like him. He was such a two-timing villain. But, of course, you see how that worked out for him."

"Where is he now?" Adriana desperately tried to remain calm. If she could keep Sarah Jane talking, perhaps she could get to Adam.

217

"In hell, probably, would be my supposition." Sarah Jane laughed. "Did you think he got up and walked away after he was stabbed?"

"His body disappeared."

"His very *heavy* body was dragged into the woods for the wild animals to feast on. I hoped you would think him alive and still a threat. And, I have no doubt you did. And so will everyone else when you are found dead. There will be no doubt in anyone's mind that he was responsible."

"What do you want, Sarah Jane?"

"Why, I wish you to die, of course."

Adriana took a deep breath. "I understand. Can I not just offer you money since this is what you obviously desire?"

"It is too late for that. I do not want some of the Booth wealth, my dear. I want it all. It should have been mine."

"You are right. My father did a terrible thing. He did provide you with a stipend, but it was clearly not enough."

"Then why did you not offer to make things right? I had to leave my home. I was cast into impoverishment. You could have stepped aside when the will was read."

"You are right. It was my mistake. I should have and I did not. Can you forgive me? I wish to correct the situation now. I can give you this house and the money. It will all be yours. Just give me my son."

Sarah Jane thought for a moment, then lifted the sleeping babe nearly into Adriana's outstretched arms. But, then she pulled the child back and cuddled him against her chest. "How do I know you are not lying to me? If I give you back the brat, I will have no means to see you keep your word."

"Paul Kernley is downstairs. I can call him. He can

prepare a document and I will sign it. I will give you anything. All that you ask and more. Just, please, give me my child."

Sarah Jane thought for a moment. "No. Jason betrayed me and you will, too. I can trust no one. I must kill you."

"How did Jason betray you? By telling me it was you who shot at me? He admitted he was responsible."

She laughed. "That part was all his idea. He thought if you felt threatened, you would turn to him. But, it made you trust him less. So, he followed you to bring you back. He promised me he would kill you and I would inherit. Then, we would divide the spoils. It seemed the perfect strategy."

"You must have known he had motives all his own. You are too smart to give him the upper hand. Why did you not merely finish me yourself in the beginning? It makes no sense."

"So simple, really. After the reading of the will, I'll admit I was a bit distraught. I took shelter at Jason's old wreck of a property. He arrived home and caught me there. I told him what happened and he offered sympathy. And a solution. One that would be profitable for us both. He seemed to like killing, but I do not fancy it. And I knew Jason would betray me. It was his nature. Your husband did me a huge favor when he ended Jason's life. And so it is perfect, after all."

"You could have come to me. All this intrigue was not necessary."

"You little bitch. You would not have helped me. You hated me."

"No, Sarah Jane. I wanted to like you. You seemed to have no desire to be close to me. I was but a child when my mother died. I looked to you for that relationship."

"It is of no consequence now."

"How can I make this right?"

"I told you. Die." She shrugged as if it was the simplest of answers.

"If that is the price for the safety of my son, then so be it. Just put him back in his cradle and I shall go with you."

"Oh, you will go with me. He comes, too. He is my guarantee you will do as I say."

"But why hurt him? He is an innocent."

"I do not care a whit about the brat. Once you are dead, I shall abandon him and someone will stumble upon him. If he is meant to survive, then he will."

Adriana desperately tried to find a reason for Sarah Jane to believe she would cooperate without putting Adam at risk. This was a mother's worst nightmare.

Thinking quickly, she surreptitiously released the clasp on her new necklace. It fell silently to the carpet.

Sarah Jane stood up, still holding Adam against her chest. The child slept and Adriana was grateful. Sarah Jane indicated for Adriana to follow and Adriana meekly walked behind the woman. They moved down the corridor to the servants' staircase. At the front of the house, the party was in full revelry and the sounds drifted up as they descended.

Sarah Jane led her out the back and they walked across the grounds.

"Can I just hold him a moment? He will be chilled. The night air is cold."

"Do you believe me so naïve or gullible that I would so easily give up my leverage? It is not so cold. We will be out of the night air soon enough."

"Where are we going?"

The Hadley property loomed before them. Adriana shivered. She ran through one excuse after another to try and wrest the child from Sarah Jane's grasp, but she could come up with nothing that would not put Adam in danger.

Be calm. That is your only hope. You can figure a way to save him. Oh, please, Robert, come looking for me. Find us. Save us.

Chapter Thirty-Eight

Still laughing at some silly jest, Robert climbed the stairs in search of his wife. She had gone to check on Adam, but that had been a while ago. He was sorely missing her and wondered as to the delay. As he entered the nursery, he sensed something was amiss.

It was empty.

Adam was not in his cradle and Adriana was nowhere in sight. Robert moved forward and his foot caught on something. The necklace he had given Adriana earlier that evening! How strange. Adriana was not a careless person and would have missed the piece if it had loosened. He examined the clasp and found it intact. This was deliberate. Quelling the terror that threatened to choke him, he sprang into action.

Springing into action, he ran from the room as if demons chased him. He had been near the front staircase and would have noticed her descent, so he tore down the hallway to the back stairs. Taking them three at a time, he nearly ran Martha over at the bottom. She was clearly panicked.

"Where?"

Martha pointed out the back. "It was Sarah Jane," she spit out, "I was just coming for you."

"Get Tate." He flew outside.

Tate caught up with him. They stealthily slipped through the darkness to the looming ghost of Hadley house. A wisp of candlelight flickered through an opening. They approached cautiously. They had been together a long time and their communication was wordless. Tate went around one side and Robert the other.

***

"There must be some solution to this, Sarah Jane. You do not wish to be a murderess. You have said as much. I know we have not always been close, but do you really wish my death? Or to harm my child?"

Sarah Jane just stared at her. Before she could answer, Adam let out his lusty cries.

"Shut up," Sarah Jane snapped at the babe. She turned to Adriana. "Make him stop. I cannot stand that noise. It pierces my very soul. Shut him up or I shall."

"He is merely hungry. Just let me feed him and he will quiet. I beg of you. You are right here and can watch. I will give him back as soon as he is satisfied. If I am to die this night, what can it hurt to let me have this last moment with my child?"

Adam continued to exercise his lungs and Sarah Jane thrust the child at Adriana. "I do not care what you do so long as you make him stop that terrible shrieking."

With great relief, Adriana exposed her breast. The boy sucked with gusto. Adriana held him for what she feared was the very last time. Her eyes filled with tears. She adored this little boy. She did not want that horrible woman to lay hands on her beloved son again. But, what could she do? Reason was her only hope.

"Sarah Jane, I shall give you anything you wish.

Anything. Money, the manor, anything. Just spare us. That is all I ask."

"Can you make him love me?"

"Who?"

"Daniel. Your father. Can you? He could not love me. He only loved your mother. I tried, but it was as if I did not even exist."

"That is what all of this is about? My father?"

"He promised to love me, but he lied. He drank himself into a stupor every day of our marriage, as if to forget his life with me. Even in death, he showed his disdain for me. He left you all and I got nothing. He humiliated me. I was his wife!" This last was screamed.

"You were. It is true. He was unfair to you. I can make it right. I will give you all that is due to you. Just let us go and we will see to it this very night. You do not want our blood on your hands."

Sarah Jane seemed to hesitate for a moment, then shook her head. "Why should I trust you? You thrust me out."

"No, Sarah Jane. You left on your own. I would never have turned you out."

"You lie." Sarah Jane reached into the folds of her skirt and came out with a small pistol. It was a shock since Sarah Jane had always voiced her disdain for guns. Adriana gasped. "You know you don't wish to shoot. You have always said you are afraid of guns."

"And you believed that? You are more naïve than I thought. You never know when you must defend what is yours and no one will ever suspect I was the one wielding the weapon. Everyone knows how I feel about these." She looked down at the pistol and smiled malevolently.

"Set the child aside," Sarah Jane demanded, waving the gun in front of herself.

Carefully, Adriana laid the sleeping Adam on the floor as far behind her as she could reach.

"Promise you will leave him here untouched for his father to find."

"I owe you naught. It is you who has the debt. For that, you shall give your life. The child is nothing to me. I care not what happens to it."

Sarah Jane raised the gun and aimed it at Adriana's chest. Adriana took one last look at her sleeping son and squeezed her eyes shut. Then the world turned to chaos. The blast of the weapon echoed off the broken stones, joining with Adriana's scream and the sound of something heavy falling to the ground. The cacophony woke Adam, who began to cry loudly. Adriana was knocked down. Something landed on top of her. A voice screeched once and then it was quiet except for Adam, who continued to demand satisfaction. The heavy weight lifted from her back as hands reached down to grasp her arms. Adriana screamed, then realized it was Robert.

The next thing she knew, Adam was back in her arms and she was rocking him, tears spilling on him like drops of rain. Robert was with her and her son was in her arms and all was right with the world.

"I did not mean to hit her so hard," Tate said, not sounding apologetic. "She is dead."

Robert shrugged. "She deserved no less. I am not sorry." He turned to Adriana. "Are you well, my love?"

"Yes. Thanks to you both. How did you know?"

"I found the necklace. It was a clever clue. And then Martha saw you leaving with Sarah Jane. Thank God you both are safe."

"Again you have slain the dragon for me, sir knight."

"It is my own life I saved, my lady. For I would certainly die without you."

"What of my help?' Tate asked, sounding hurt.

"You are my other hero, as always. We are eternally grateful. Are we not, Robert?"

"I suppose you were of benefit," Robert allowed.

Seemingly disgusted, Tate shook his head. "If I could but count the times I have protected your back. I have the scars to prove it."

Epilogue

It was a different voyage this time. A year had passed since the last time Robert and Adriana had made this crossing, but the accommodations were much changed. A cradle had been built into the captain's cabin and nailed securely to the wooden planks. It was another member of the crew, the elevated cabin boy, who slept in the galley storage room. He was to give aid to the new cook. This trip, it was Cassie who supervised the kitchen. Tate would tolerate no more of tasteless fare and knew his new bride would see that this did not occur. The captain had his bed widened to accommodate the addition of his lovely bride. Additional comforts were added, like a rocking chair.

Robert came up with the idea that it should be Tate continuing some of the voyages back and forth to England, with Cassie seeing to it the men had bellies filled with delicious food. The route was too profitable to merely abandon. Robert had properties to see to and even thought he might consider entering local politics. Change was coming in the colonies and he found the idea of being part of it intriguing. Tate would never be happy spending all of his time on land so it was a perfect solution.

Adriana spent much of her time holding her precious babe. Robert walked with them on deck, inhaling the bracing sea air, and telling his son tales of angels and mermaids and magic. He slipped in a story or two of sea monsters for balance. The babe was delighted when his father spoke, smiling at the sound. "A born captain," Robert said with pride.

"I think not," Adriana responded. "Captains drink too much rum and get themselves in trouble."

"My love, if you are the kind of problems captains encounter, then I wish him nothing more than a life at sea."

Nights were spent wrapped in each other's arms, savoring the nearness and the love they shared. Adam blissfully slept through the nights, the ocean rocking him in pleasant dreams.

The day they landed in Virginia was cause for celebration. Robert was anxious to show off Adam to his mother. Tate and Cassie were impatient to move into their new home and see to the arrangements for returning to sea. Robert and Adriana were still negotiating as to the price for the cottage.

As they arrived at Robert's house, Adriana was suddenly overcome with a feeling of wellbeing. It felt like she was coming home. As they approached, the sound of a dog barking filled the air. "Blossom?" Adriana called.

She handed Adam to Robert and fairly jumped from the carriage. A large, tawny dog approached her suspiciously, then caught her scent and nearly knocked her over with enthusiasm. Adriana wrapped her arms about the now-huge creature and buried her face in the soft neck. Blossom licked her face, her neck, wherever her tongue could reach. It was a joyous reunion.

The front portal swung open. Elizabeth Stuart ran down the steps to greet them and Adriana watched as the child was held and coddled. Hazel appeared, wrapped her arms around Adriana and Robert and reached for Adam.

"Another Stuart to raise up. My work is never done."

Adriana caught her eye and mouthed a "thank you" indicating the dog. Hazel just smiled. "Cinnamon?" she asked the older woman.

"In the stables. Grown fat from lack of exercise."

"I will see to that problem. I can never thank you enough."

"Thank God you is all safe," Hazel said. "The Lord does answer prayers."

"If only you could learn to cook," sighed Elizabeth. "I have been praying for that for years." They all laughed at that, until even Hazel had to join in.

Adriana took a deep breath. It had indeed been a journey thus far, but the best was just beginning.

About the Author

Leslie Hachtel has been working since she was fifteen and her various jobs have included licensed veterinary technician, caterer, horseback riding instructor for the disabled and advertising media buyer, which have all given her a wealth of experiences.

However, it has been writing that has consistently been her passion. She is an award-winning and Amazon bestselling author who has written seventeen romance novels, including twelve historicals and five romantic suspense.

Leslie lives in Florida with her very supportive husband, and her writing buddy, Josie, the poodle mix.

She loves to hear from readers!

Website: https://www.lesliehachtel.com/
Facebook: https://www.facebook.com/lesliehachtelwriter/
Twitter: @lesliehachtel
Blog: http://lesliehachtelwriter.wordpress.com
Bookbub: https://www.bookbub.com/authors/leslie-hachtel

Made in United States
Orlando, FL
19 January 2024